Praise

"The message is cle____ young people to truly live according to their beliefs, stand firmly on their own ground and not merely be a follower in the crowd."

Mentor Magazine

"A very courageous account of what it means to be a young person today. Hoover focuses on the importance of relationships, of staying in school, of fair play and setting positive goals. This is truly a story of self-respect and friendship woven with intelligence and maturity."

William C. Pratella, Ph. D
Superintendent of Schools—Mt. Vernon, NY

"*My Friend, My Hero* is worth anyone's investment in the reading arena. It speaks not only to young hearts, but to all hearts, all ages and stages."

Rev. Dr. Cecil L. "Chip" Murray
F.A.M.E. Church, Los Angeles, CA

"There's a little comedy, a little drama, a little suspense and a little mystery with the end result being...a story that is not only entertaining, but enlightening...*My Friend My Hero* is a wonderful first novel."

Blackboard African-American Bestsellers, Inc.

"Congratulations on your remarkable book. It reaches into the soul and [it is] something that every young person should read. This book shows your remarkable ability as a writer. In my opinion, you deserve the Pulitzer Prize."

Lady D. Madison
United House of Prayer

"A candid story of life and death. *My Friend, My Hero* could be a fine tool for analytical problem solving dialog in any contemporary classroom."

Marcia de Chadenedes
Centrum Education Programs

"I was glued...fascinated."

Ronald A. Blackwood
Mayor of the City of Mount Vernon

"Kudos goes to Jerald Levon Hoover for giving voice to the concerns which face our youth."

Chicago Defender

"... like an overdue trip down memory lane with a powerful message!...REAL!...It's first class fiction with a message its reader cannot ignore!"

Bill Daughtry
WFAN Radio

"The style in which Mr. Hoover writes takes you back to the beginning and allows you to be brought into the future with a clear understanding of the world that these young unsung heroes are from. We see success measured in a new way."

J. E. Alson-Johnson
James Weldon Johnson Community Centers, Inc.

"The lack of profanity and illicit connotations through out the entire novel and the strong anti-drug and Stay in School message is in itself a very unique and refreshing experience."

Saint Louis Sentinel

"...transcends age and racial barriers ... ENTERTAINING ... REALISTIC ... a 'must read' novel for parents, teachers, students...anyone whose life has been touched or will be touched by drugs, alcohol abuse, violence, or the many other evils that plague our society and our youth."

Sacramento Observer

"Reading this novel filled me with excitement and enthusiasm ... *My Friend, My Hero* isn't just the average novel with a strong positive message ... it gives you an insight on true friendship and a longing to do right things."

Atlanta Daily World

"There is an emerging voice in this land which rings with the collective energy of the thousands of Black Americans who are awakening to the healing potential found in deep race introspection. Jerald Levon Hoover has joined with this great chorus in producing a work that seems in the wake of the Million Man March to be prophetic in its scope and emphasis."

Michigan Chronicle

HE WAS MY HERO, TOO

Jerald Levon Hoover

UPStream Publication

Brooklyn, New York
11238

Published by

UpStream Publication

a division of A&B Publishers Group
1000 Atlantic Avenue
Brooklyn, New York
11238
http://www.anbdonline.com

He Was My Hero Too © 2002 by Jerald Levon Hoover. All rights reserved. No part of this book may be reproduced in any form or by any means including electronic, mechanical or photocopying or stored in a retrieval system without permission in writing from the publisher except by a reviewer who may quote brief passages to be included in a review.

COVER ILLUSTRATION: © *Andre Harris*
TYPESETTING & INTERIOR DESIGN: *Industrial Fonts & Graphix*

Library of Congress Cataloging-In-Publication

Hoover, Jerald Le Von, 1965-
 He was my hero too/Jerald Le Von Hoover
  p. cm.
 ISBN: 1-886433-78-X (alk paper)
  1. Mount Vernon (Westchester County, N.Y.)—Fiction. 2. African American teenagers—Fiction. 3. African American families—Fiction. 4. Drug abuse—Fiction. I. Title

PS3558. 06332 H4 2002
813 .54—dc21   2002027984

Manufactured & Printed in the Canada
04 05 06 10 9 8 7 6 5 4 3 2

To my little "hero"...
My son, Jordan

FOREWORD

OVER THE course of my years, I have been impressed with the abilities of those who were able to rise above what many would predict to be their futures. They confounded the so-called experts and overcame the odds.

Such a young man as the author, Jerald Levon Hoover, by all accounts statistically should have failed. He saw a world that chewed up and spit out so many people that he knew and loved. He saw a world desperate and unfeeling, but he also saw a world of opportunity, one that sent a message that all things are possible if you just believe.

Over a period of time, having had developed a relationship with this young man, I discovered that he had the temerity to succeed, to overcome the odds. Jerald Levon Hoover knew the one common message recurrent in so many people's lives—a willingness to humble themselves and chase a *spirit*. He chose the spirit that fortified his existence. One that enabled him to reach out, making way for strength and character. He chose a *spirit* that allowed him to avoid the familiar path of destruction and despair. He chose a *spirit* that allowed him to climb mountains and to see the star of success.

This young spirit has gone back in time; giving back, recording his experiences in book form. Perhaps as we read this book it will serve to instruct us to live out our lives with even more purpose, more determination and more direction.

Jerald Levon Hoover chose a spirit that allowed him to overcome the odds, and he has done this knowing there will be a better tomorrow.

Ernest D. Davis
Mayor of Mount Vernon, N.Y.

A City That Believes

INTRODUCTION

EVOLVING! ONGOING! Everlasting feelings are the transcending thoughts, energies, and spirits of our elders and ancestors from our community, Mount Vernon, New York—a.k.a the *City on the Move* and *A City That Believes*.

Our elders and ancestors transcending voices are crying out, *and still I will rise!*

Jerald Levon Hoover expresses his inner most thoughts, emotions and fears in this literary work. What is also expressed is his love for God, himself, his family and the community of Mount Vernon. His concerns encompass the social ills that have plagued this community, its parents and definitely the youth of today and of the past.

Yes...*and still I will rise!*

What is quite intriguing, unique, heartwarming and fascinating about, *He Was My Hero, Too* and of course, *My Friend, My Hero* is the setting, Mount Vernon, N.Y. where Jerald Levon Hoover decided to develop his characters and story-line around an average African-American family struggling and surviving to move forward. The places such as, the Levister Towers (the projects), the high school, the South-side Boys and Girls Club and the local churches of Third Street and Sixth and Ninth Avenues are all landmarks of Mount Vernon. Those of us who know and are familiar with these places can truly appreciate and understand Jerald Levon Hoover's vision. This is an expression that will have an impact on our youth, their families and their communities. To which incidentally, are still struggling with the same social issues: drugs, alcohol, teenage pregnancy, AIDS, lack of education, unemployment – along with the Basketball Jones.' Yes...*and still I will rise!*

The city of Mount Vernon, with a population of over 80,000 within its four square miles, is a great city. Many cultural, ethnic groups have a profound effect on the greatness of this city. Since the beginning of the twentieth century, African-Americans, Jews, Italians, and many other cultures have made contributions that stand out. These cultures or ethnic groups by and large exemplify the rich heritage and strong history that Mount Vernon now proclaims.

I would like to share a few thoughts praising the contributions of African-Americans and their vital roles in the rich heritage of Mount Vernon. I am not taking away from any other culture or ethnic group because their influence is equally honorable and well represented. I am—for over 40 years—very much a part of all of

He Was My Hero, Too

them. I am an African-American who is very proud of the evolution, growth and development of our race and the vital roles we've played in the past and present. Today my deep emotions are driven by the voices of the elders, ancestors and my experiences as a Mount Vernonite. I often remind people that you can go across this country far and wide and you will not find another city quite like Mount Vernon—a city that can share and boast of a legacy of successful people in every profession. You can name it from: politics, education, the arts and entertainment, sports, medicine, the military, writers, the clergy and human services. Again, you can name it and an African-American from Mount Vernon has achieved it. Denzel Washington—himself a Mount Vernonite and a product of the South-side Boys and Girls Club—while accepting his historic Academy Award made mention of Mount Vernon. This is something he does often whenever he is interviewed. The phenomenon is that many of these Mount Vernonites were born and raised in Levister Towers, "the projects." They graduated from Mount Vernon High School, and also were members of the local Boys and Girls Clubs, (North and South-side units), as well as the churches in the area. Yes...*and still I will rise!*

There have been four public schools renamed in Mount Vernon from prominent national figures. Three were Mount Vernonites and one an African from the continent of Africa. These schools were so renamed from Robert Fulton to Edward Williams; Nathan Hale to Cecil Parker; George Washington to Nellie Thorton and James Grimes to Nelson Mandela. These successful achievements pay homage to the elders and ancestors and unsung heroes from the 20's, 30's, 40's and 50's; whose sole desires were that their children, *would work hard and grow up to be somebody.* A recipe that was very simple. Guess what? It worked!

In the late 80's a book entitled, *A Time To Remember,* written by Larry H. Spruill, H.D. the Mount Vernon historian documented the first comprehensive study with photographs of the African-American community from the very beginning (late 1800's) through the 1980's. Dr. Spruill is one of those Mount Vernonites, like Jerald Levon Hoover that was raised and grew up in the, and I quote, "the projects."

Yes! Yes! Yes! And still I will rise!

When you become familiar with the place and setting and get to look at some history of Mount Vernon, *all ethnic groups* included, you will truly understand and appreciate Jerald Levon Hoover's work as a writer.

Jerald Levon Hoover had a strong commitment to express his ability to inspire one to take a look at their own lives, its issues, pressures and circumstances and still say, a*nd still I will rise.* I did not have the opportunity to interact *personally* and share experiences with Jerald Levon Hoover as a young man growing up in Mount Vernon. However, I did share experiences with his strong and courageous mother, Hilda Hoover and several members of his loving and close-knit family.

But, now, because of the transcending spirits and energies of the past from families living "in the projects," the opportunity has allowed me to get to know Jerald Levon Hoover and share in his creative expression. Jerald Levon Hoover is carrying out the call of the elders and ancestors from this great city, Mount Vernon.

It is my hope that you will enjoy reading this novel and that you will gain a vivid understanding of its most essential message.

Yes! Yes! Yes! I have risen again, and again and yet again! These are the voices of the elders and ancestors. It is through them that we continue to live and grow.

This belief in the oneness of humankind, about which have often spoken in concerts and elsewhere, has existed within me side by side with my deep attachment to the cause of my own race. I do not think, however, that my sentiments are contradictory...there truly is a kinship among us all, a basis for mutual respect and brotherly love. —Paul Robeson

William (Billy) Thomas
Former Executive Director
Mount Vernon Boys & Girls Club

ONE

THE SILKY SMOOTH sound of legendary jazz saxophonist, John Coltrane, permeated from the Voice of Music phonograph. Simon sat in deep meditation behind the desk in his office at the South-side Mount Vernon Boys & Girls Club and soaked it all in. Simon, a portly and bearded man with a tinge of gray hair, was dressed in a dark brown velvet warm-up suit, which offset the colors of his new digs—the log cabin. Simon's office attracted the nickname by club members when he personally had his office renovated with all wood fixtures.

The sole piece of accessory not made of maple was the "wall of fame" where Simon kept the snapshots of every athlete who ever grace the club's gymnasium and went on to the professional ranks. He also had a space where he kept the entire club's, "hall of fame" honorees.

Simon's focus was broken by a knock on the door. It was Kirby, sporting shorts, hi-top Chuck Taylor Converse sneakers, and droopy socks, with a white towel draped around his neck. Simon, pleased by the familiar voice, swirled around to greet his visitor. The two gentlemen smiled, then embraced.

"Man, I haven't seen you in a month of Sundays." Simon, the club's program coordinator, said while shutting off the music that stirred his soul.

"Yeah, I know, IBM had me in the frozen tundra, Chicago, doing seminars—and I've been dealing with a few things which sort of needed my immediate and absolute attention."

"I can dig it, Mr. Computer Consultant."

"So how've you been?"

"Me?" Simon smiled and patted on his ever-expanding balloon belly, "I've been making it just fine. You know, another day, another fifty cents."

"You're a trip," Kirby said.

"So," Simon's voice shifted, "how's life in White Plains?"

"It's all right, considering. I really don't do too much there, just work and sleep." Kirby sucked in some air and sighed. "It's especially hard not seeing Junior and Bennie every day."

Simon pointed to the photo of Kirby's family positioned on his desk. "And what about Kathy, your wife?"

Kirby makes an impulsive about-face and shoved his hands into his pockets to jingle with his change. "Yeah," he moaned. "I almost forgot, her too."

"Hang in there, you guys will be all right."

"I think we're headed for divorce court, if you ask me."

He Was My Hero, Too

"Well no, I didn't ask you," Simon said with a sly grin. "You'll see, it'll come around. A year's separation after nine years of marriage isn't the end of the world. Just look at it as a refreshing period—a cleansing period."

"Cleansing? Refreshing?" Kirby questioned. "I'd say it's more like an emotional enema."

"Enema?"

"I don't know," Kirby said and shook his head in disagreement. "Women's be buggin'. It's like a light goes off in their head and they just...flip! First they get our ribs, now they take our paychecks!"

"Man," Simon sounded a little more reticent as he picked up the telephone. "Simon speaking, can you hold please?" He placed his hand over the receiver to muzzle the sound. "You better not go anywhere in public talking that stuff."

"What? About my wife?"

"No, about the ribs and money."

The door swung open as if a hurricane wind had gotten a hold of it. It was Dannon, clad in a white Adidas sweat suit and matching white sneakers.

"I need a ball, Bra Simon."

"You forget how to knock, man?" Simon said as he was just about to conclude his telephone conversation.

"Oh, I apologize, Simon. Kirby, what's up?"

"Nothing. Yo boy, how tall are you now?"

"Six-eight."

"It's only been a couple of weeks since I last saw you, and you put on two more inches?"

"I don't know, I guess."

Kirby shook his head in astonishment, thinking of how it felt like just yesterday when he use to give Dannon piggyback rides.

"Whew! And you're seventeen now?"

"Yep, turn eighteen, June 10th."

"I know when your birthday is chump."

Dannon playfully landed an elbow to Kirby's chest. "Well, I gotta roll, gotta shoot some hoop; keep my jumper on target."

"When's the next game?" Kirby yelled down the corridor.

"Thursday! Big game against New Ro!"

Kirby made his way back into Simon's office. His thoughts drifted to his best friend Bennett, Dannon's older brother. He thought about how much he still missed him with every passing day. And the thought of how proud Bennett would have been of Dannon, who took over from where he left off—touted as the best basketball player Mount Vernon High School had ever produced.

Dannon had the same physical lineaments as Bennett—tall and lean with a wingspan of a seven-footer. And compared to Bennett, Dannon had those catcher's-mitt type hands that empowered him to grip and palm a basketball with just his thumb and ring finger. He wore a real close haircut; the way Bennett had sported his. And although two-inches taller and twenty pounds heavier, his strut was similar to Bennett's.

He Was My Hero, Too

They had this confident swagger about them on the court that said, "when I'm on top of my game, no one can guard me." The one major difference between them was Dannon shot the ball left-handed. This was until Dannon—so crazy about the way his big brother played, qualified himself to shoot with his right hand. Hence, affording him the luxury of shooting from long distance and with deadly accuracy with either hand—a feat not done by many who played the game. One sportswriter nicknamed him "Idaho," his colloquialism for potato. The writer cited the various ways of eating the Idaho potato: mashed, chipped, sliced, boiled, baked, and fried, to name a few—to the many facets of Dannon's game. Any time he took to the court, he was simply a man among boys; a king among kings; a lord among—well maybe not quite that—but you get the idea. Simply put, the young man was awesome.

So much has changed since their days in high school: the town, the people, the school, just about everything. The town of Mount Vernon elected its first Jewish mayor, Sol Weiss, a former high school classmate. The former class nerd who became an efficacious politician is happily married to an African-American woman.

But drugs have besieged the old neighborhood: crack, angel dust, heroin, you name it. Young people ten, eleven, and twelve-years-old are committing heinous crimes. The wholesomeness that was once a trademark of the suburban town, just 10 miles north of

New York City, had given way to community neglect, disregard for life and lost hope. Not to anyone's surprise, some of the local dailies started calling Mount Vernon, "Little Columbia."

"What happened to this place?" Kirby asked while studying the pictures.

"What, the club?"

"No," Kirby shook his head and squinted as if he were fending off sunlight, "this city."

"Well..."

"I was born and raised here. My mother is still here, my wife and kids..."

"Listen, Kirby," Simon said affirmatively, "times change, people change. I mean—if anyone is an authority on the subject, it's definitely me."

Simon's own metamorphosis was an affirmation. He went from being a numbers-runner, dope pusher, and pimp to becoming an upstanding well-respected elder of the community. One who became a loving, faithful husband, and devoted stepfather.

Of course, as Simon would tell it, it would not have been possible without finding Jesus Christ as his Lord and personal Savior while serving five years behind bars. And after his release, Simon answered what he perceived as his calling and became an ordained fire and brimstone Baptist preacher.

Simon met his soul mate, LoNelle, who was at the time a nurse and a single mother of one daughter, through an "Adopt a Prisoner Pen-Pal" program spon-

He Was My Hero, Too

sored by her church.

LoNelle was a ravishing woman with huge dimples and short salt and pepper hair. She had the prettiest hazel eyes that blended nicely with her lightly freckled skin. She was tall with very long legs. In high heels, she towered over Simon, and everyone else for that matter. But he could care less; for he knew as provocative as she was, it was only a benefit to look up to her.

Simon's regal character also gave birth to a new nickname, "Bra Simon" by many of the locals who cited his tireless work with wayward youths as well as adults. He developed and funded a program, 'Brotherhood Night,' a lecture and discussion held every Wednesday at the Boys Club. Women were allowed to come; just not encouraged. Thus, they were there anyway.

"Why don't you come out to Brotherhood Night, tomorrow?"

Kirby shot paper balls into the trashcan and pretended he was his favorite NBA player—Magic Johnson—unleashed a deep sigh, "I don't know."

"Come, and bring the boys, they'll enjoy it."

"You still tell those corny jokes at the end of each meeting? I heard about them."

"Some things never change. And besides, my jokes aren't corny, thank you."

"Yeah, yeah."

"Man, are you all right?"

"Yeah, I'm fine."

"Why are you holding your head? You're still getting

those headaches, aren't you? You better get yourself checked out."

"Please, Simon, change the subject. Tell me a joke or something."

Simon sat back and thought, as if a beam of light just shone upon him, snapped his fingers, and said, "You've just reminded me, I have a good one to tell you. This is a real knee-slapper."

"My headache is gone now...see?"

"Sit down."

"Oh, brother," Kirby sat and braced himself as if he were sitting in a spacecraft awaiting takeoff.

"Two preachers—Reverend Smith and Reverend Jones—both from fairly small churches, met for their weekly lunch. 'Smitty,' Jones said, 'you look troubled. What's the matter?'

'Well,' Smitty answered. 'It seems my watch is missing.'

'You mean the handsome gold one given to you by the Bishop?' Jones asked.

'Yeah, that's it, that's the one. And what's worse is, I fear it may be someone from my congregation who took it while they were visiting me. It pains me to know that there is someone in my own church who cannot be trusted. And, I would like to know who.'

'I'll tell you what,' Jones offered, 'here's what you do. Next Sunday give a sermon on the Ten Commandments, a real fire and brimstone one. Then, when you get to *Thou Shalt Not Steal*, look out over the entire congregation. I'm certain you will be able to spot the guilty person.'

"The following week, the two Rev's meet for lunch again. 'Smitty,' Jones said, 'I see you've got your watch back. So my suggestion worked?'

'Well, in a way.'

'How do you mean in a way?'

'You see,' Smitty said. 'As I was preaching the Commandments and got to the part about, *Thou Shalt Not Commit Adultery*, I suddenly remembered where I'd left it.'"

"You're a sick man, Simon. You're not well."

"Aw, a little humor doesn't hurt anybody."

Kirby tried to fix himself from the laugh by holding his mouth shut for several seconds. But it was to no avail. It had run its course.

"How come you don't have your meetings at Grace Baptist Church?" Kirby asked when he came back to his senses. "It would be less expensive."

Simon gave the question some thought, smiled, leaned back in his chair, and swirled around. "Because money—isn't a real issue or object to me right now. Besides, it would then seem like it's a religious thing; not a social thing. And the Jews, more than likely, wouldn't come. The Catholics wouldn't come, nor the Episcopalians, Methodist, Pentecostals, Protestants, Muslims, nor anyone of any other denomination for that matter."

Simon tapped on his desk then said, "I want them all here. All are welcome."

Kirby sat as quietly as possible wrestling with a mixture of negative feelings: guilt, anger, bitterness, and confusion. As it was going on in his head, he offered in defense, "look, I didn't forget where I came from. I'm just..."

"I never ever, implied..."

"And, I, definitely didn't forget I'm Black."

"Now, Kirby, you know, I never said..."

"I mean," Kirby shook his head with disapprobation. "Mount Vernon—this place really gives me the creeps. You know, twelve years...twelve years have passed and Bennett's killer has not been found yet. I just don't understand it. I don't get it."

"Well..."

"And what's with the crackerjack police department?"

"Come on Kirby," Simon said sympathetically, "lighten up some. They did the best they knew how. They questioned everybody, particularly me."

"But he was shot in broad daylight, broad daylight!"

"Yeah...I know how you feel."

Kirby wiped his spectacles clean and walked over to peruse Simon's wall. "Every time I see this picture of Bennett, it gets to me. I don't know; I just miss my partner. He should be playing and making millions in the NBA, not lying cold in the grave in Valhalla."

"God's will," Simon said.

"Yeah, yeah."

Simon again swirled around—only this time he got

up and joined Kirby. "In a sense, he was my hero too, somebody I wish I could've been like." Simon patted Kirby on the shoulder and retreated to his seat.

"Hey, Simon, what was with the patch on the eye back then?"

Simon peered over his glasses and offered, "My M.O. and my trademark."

Kirby had to laugh at that one but then he noticed something he hadn't seen before on Simon's wall. "A master's degree in psychology from Kent State? Simon Timothy Diamond—class of '71. This is yours, man?"

"That's me."

"But, why in the world..."

"Did I live my life in the way I did?"

"Yeah."

"I just lost my way," Simon answered matter-of-factly. "It was the sixties and early seventies. And as you know, were very turbulent times for Black people. You could make an argument we—Black people—lost a savior when President Kennedy was gunned down. And, you could probably make a case for his brother, Robert, who suffered the same fate—shot dead, five years after him. But, after Dr. King was murdered—and this is after Medger was assassinated—shot in the back outside his very own home. Remember, Malcolm X got killed—for what he stood for, and a host of other civil rights activists were jailed, savagely beaten or killed. I just plain and simple gave up. And, I was there at Kent State in 1970 when National Guardsmen shot and killed those students demonstrating on campus in protest of the Vietnam War. I was within 100 feet of one of the students shot."

Simon took a moment and peeked out the window and into the cloudy rain filled skies. "My degrees meant nothing to me."

"Nothing?"

"It meant something in terms of me being the first in my family to have gotten so far. But, in terms of society and mankind, I just didn't care anymore. I used the talent or gift as a psychologist in a negative way. I got people—men and women—to do what I wanted them to do. Whether it was running numbers, pushing dope, prostitution, you name it. They did it. I owned them and controlled them."

"Man, Simon."

"Yeah, I was bad...horrible."

"You were a monster."

Simon picked up an eraser and tossed it in Kirby's direction. But, Kirby managed to duck out of harm's way.

"But, you know something?" Simon offered. "I got them all off and cleaned out."

"Really? Get outta here."

"No really. Believe it or not, all of my regular customers, I got them cleaned up and a few of them go to church regularly."

"I can believe it, you do have a way of persuasion about you."

"Yeah," Simon said. "But, I couldn't get Bennett hooked. He was a strong young man—strong."

"He had no choice," Kirby said flatly and stared menacingly at Simon. "I would've killed you both."

"Whoa, Kirby, I'm on your side now."

"I know."

The resurrected Simon allowed his emotions to get the better of him as he thought of something in his past, then said, "I did lose one. A young sister from my home state, Ohio; she was a nurse. She didn't have any family here, made good money, but had it hard growing up." Simon tried to mask his emotions but his resistance would not cooperate. Kirby shoved Simon a wooded box with tissues in it. "I tried hard to get her cleaned up, but it was too late, she was gone. She hooked and died from an overdose." Simon shook his head in disbelief. "Sometimes, I wake up in cold sweats. Half the time, I'm scaring my wife half to death because out of the blue, I start crying."

"Crying, huh?"

"Her name was Wanda. She was a beautiful, God-fearing, Christian girl. I took advantage, and now her blood I know is on my hands."

Having it hard was an understatement; nothing Wanda did was good enough for her parents. Not an only child, she had a younger brother and her parents seemed to love him more. She had to pay her own way to New York, find her own place to stay, and pay her own way through school working two jobs.

Her parents turned deaf ears to an invitation to come to her graduation. And after they discovered her cause of death, they forbade Simon's pastor from having the funeral in his church.

The couple arrived in New York, identified the body, and had a rinky-dink ceremony in a funeral parlor. They also negated to take her body back to Ohio, however, she was buried in New York.

The two men sat in respectful silence for a time. Simon reminisced regrettably over his past. His mind, wandered toward an old friend, Willie, who served as his driver and bodyguard. He was his brute-in-shining armor. Willie was gunned down—shot in the face six times—the previous year, answering to the cry of a woman being beaten by her boyfriend.

Kirby, at this time, stared intensely at a picture of Bennett slam-dunking two opponents during their high school championship title game. "Simon," Kirby said. "I want to find Bennett's killer. I really do."

"You what?"

"I'm serious, man. I want to find out who murdered Bennett. He was killed in cold-blood, and I want to know who did it."

"Why? Because you want to kill whoever did it?"

"Right now," Kirby said, giving the question some thought, "the way I feel, I'll kill whoever it is. Tomorrow, on the other hand, after I've slept on it and had a chance to be alone, I probably wouldn't. I just want justice. I want the killer caught."

Kirby walked over to the window and stared out into

the abyss.

"But..."

"Simon," Kirby said and snapped his fingers. "You still have connections in the streets, don't you?"

"Of course. I still have peoples."

"Will you help?"

"I'll make a few phone calls. But I think the mayor can help us even more."

Kirby shook his head vigorously in a "no" gesture. Simon then added, "You'll have to find the strength to get over it. I know how you feel about him, but he is the mayor and he may be privy to vital information."

"I don't know about him."

Moments later, Dannon limped into the office. "Bra Simon, Kirby, I hurt my ankle."

"You all right, man? What happened?" Kirby asked.

"I'm okay," Dannon said as he sat down in a chair provided to him by Simon. "I think I just turned it. I came down on it wrong after goin' up for a dunk."

"Sit tight," Simon said. "Let's have a look at it, then we'll see if you need to go to the hospital."

With Kirby's assistance, Simon unlaced Dannon's sneaker. .

Dannon winced in agony as Simon gave it a once over. Then he turned to Kirby and smiled, "Why don't you come around the house anymore, Kirby? Momma asks about you all the time."

"It's a long story, Dannon."

"What? You think I won't understand because I'm younger than you?"

"No. It's not that."

23

"We all know about you and Kathy. We still love you, Kathy and the kids. I shoot with the boys all the time."

"When I find the time, I will make the time."

"Great. Then you can give me a ride home."

"I can?"

"Yeah. You wouldn't want the star of the basketball team walking in the freezing cold with a bum ankle that could stiffen up, would you?"

"Kid," Kirby said as he placed his hand across Dannon's broad shoulder, "you certainly developed your brother's logic."

"Jumpshot, too."

The two shared a hearty chuckle.

"Hi, Honey," LoNelle dressed elegantly, appeared and greeted her husband with a kiss on the lips. In a flash, the office forfeited its reek of sweat and cruddy gymnasium odor and gave way to the alluring scent of Channel No. 5 perfume.

"Hi, Darlin'," Simon said and returned a kiss of his own. "You're just in time—will you please take a look at Dannon's ankle?"

LoNelle knelt to get a better look and said, "Oooh, it's swollen all right, we'll need some ice."

"Tisha," Simon said through the speakerphone.

"Yes, Bra Simon."

"Bring me a bucket of ice, please."

"Comin' right up."

Simon snapped his head back in a double take at the size of Dannon's foot, and then added, "Tisha, I think you better make it a great big bucket of ice."

Two

Kirby encamped his shiny black, late model '82 fully loaded, 325i BMW up in front of Dannon's building. The Levister Tower Housing Project was a ten-story quintuplet of dark brown brick buildings. Each edifice was equipped with an incinerator that blew heavy dark smoke through the chimney every so often. An intercom system, albeit broken, was installed for security purposes and added an element of class.

Unfortunately, some of natives that lived there did not see it that way and proceeded to destroy the system whenever it was in some type of working order.

"Okay, superstar," Kirby quipped, "why don't you just limp yourself on out of my car."

"Aw, come on, you said, you'd come see Momma. Besides, you should help me upstairs. You wouldn't want my ankle to suffer any more damage, would you? I mean, not before the big game, right?"

"Of course not, but..."

"No, 'buts'," Dannon interrupted and reached over to shut off the ignition, "too much of a conjunction."

"What are you some type of English literary?"

"Nope."

"Man, you better give me back my keys."

"Not until you say, you'll come see Momma."

As Kirby looked around his old neighborhood, his stomach began to knot up. He tried looking at one of his old hangouts—a grassy diamond-shaped area where he, Bennett, and the rest of his crew used to play their version of baseball. They were so impecunious back then, they used a tennis ball and a wooden stick. But his one-time haven has since dried up and is now buried under cement and a razor fence.

Looking around, Kirby gestured to a young woman walking past them to the building. "The young girl there, isn't she Darlene, Jeff Kendall's baby sister?"

Dannon who was massaging his sore ankle, said, "yeah, all thirteen years of her."

"And she's pregnant?" Kirby said with a bit of annoyance.

"She got knocked up by some drug dealer, named 'Shoo Shoo'."

"How old is this 'Shoo Shoo' character?"

"I think around fifteen or sixteen. I know he's younger than me."

"When will these babies stop having these babies? When?"

"Man, I wish I could tell you," Dannon said and

He Was My Hero, Too

frowned thinking the question was for him.

Kirby began frantically patting his pockets then he went into his glove compartment and pulled out his wallet.

"Dannon, you still seeing the girl you introduced me to last year?"

"Diane? Yeah, kinda sort of."

"Well here, take this."

"Come on Kirby, I don't need that."

"Man, the last thing you need right now is to make a baby. You're getting ready for college and you need to be able to concentrate on your studies and playing ball. By the way, you ever decide on what school you want to attend?"

"I narrowed my choices to St. John's and Syracuse. But..."

Kirby then capriciously reverted to the old subject, "It's more than okay to have a girlfriend, but put your priorities first. And don't trust any girl telling you she's protecting herself. You protect..."

"Kirby, will you please calm down. The reason I don't need one is because I already have one," Dannon said as he went into his bag. "It's as old as can be, but I have it just in case."

"Good for you, smart man."

"Momma taught me about the so-called 'birds and the bees.' She taught me and she warned me. Matter-of-fact, she threatened me."

Dannon started laughing then uttered, "I never knew

a little bee could kill a big gigantic bird and clip his wings and have them for a snack."

"Good ol' Mrs. Wilson, God bless her."

"You can have her."

"Man," Kirby said, "I'll never forget the first time we took Junior to school. Kathy and I both, after dropping him off in class, had to race to our car so we could cry in private. It was a very proud moment for us."

"How was Bennie's first day?"

"Oh, Dannon, it was terrible."

"Terrible?"

"Yeah, terrible. We had to drag the little joker out the car. And once he got into the building, he dropped to his knees, which meant we had to drag him down the hall kicking and screaming like a mad man. I couldn't have cried if I wanted to, I was too wore out."

"That's funny."

"Say, how's your sister?"

Dannon absorbed the unpremeditated question then set loose a look of anguish.

"What's the matter? You and Yvette aren't on good terms anymore?"

"It's not me and Yvette," Dannon revealed. "I'm nuts about my big sister. I love her to death. It's her crazy husband and his wacky kids I ain't too thrilled with. I don't know why she married that clown anyway. He's not only twelve years older than her; he's been married five times and has seven kids. The youngest two brats live with them."

He Was My Hero, Too

"How does your Momma feel about him?"

"She's from the South," Dannon waved in the air. "She loves everybody. Always hollerin' 'just give him a chance.'"

"And, I guess you aren't willing to do it?"

"Hey, four strikes and you're out—give it up."

"Dannon..."

"Kirby," Dannon interceded. "The last woman he was married to was a marital counselor, slash relationship expert. You figure that one out."

"I can understand how you feel," Kirby said and let loose a smile. "But you'll have to find a way to deal with it so it won't cause a strain with you and Yvette."

"I know, I know."

"As far as relationships go, I'm certainly no expert myself. Just look at me. I'm separated from Kathy. But, I do have a theory. It may not be shared by most, though. But I think of relationships like I think of new objects—automobiles in particular."

"What do you mean?"

"Just think. When a person buys a new car, he or she cares for it like it there was no tomorrow. They won't allow eating in it. The new smell is intoxicating. They'll find themselves going to the carwash at least once a week. They'll find themselves constantly looking at the car with admiration after buffing it with a towel.

The ride down the roughest of streets feels as smooth as can be. And you practically will have to wipe off your feet before you get in. Then all of a sudden, the new smell disappears. You'll see coins or a French fry or two on the back seat, or on the floor. Instead of washing it once a week, you may wash it once a month—and only if you can find the time. When you hit a bump in the road, not only is it rocky, but also it almost feels like an earthquake. The monthly note they have to pay becomes an all-out bill. Then the car suffers its first fender bender or scratch. And don't forget the dreaded mechanical problems. After a while, the automobile has become a headache. But, low and behold and after a while, you're riding down the street and you see another car—a different and newer car. Something more pleasant and delightful to the eyes and you are more than ready to trade in what you have for something else."

"You really feel that way? You think it's really like you said?"

"Think about it. When a person meets another person they like, they can't stop thinking about them. The phone won't ring enough. Every day is sunny. Then when the rains pour and the winds of war begin to rage, they're ready to jump ship, or find someone else who's more appealing to the eyes."

"You know what they say," Dannon said with a smile. "One man's trash is another man's treasure."

"Man, that only works if you work for the Department of Sanitation."

Then the two gentlemen exploded into a boisterous laughter.

"Is that how you feel about marriage too, Bra?"

"Marriage is a little different, especially if there are kids involved. But the principles are the same. And, I personally think a lot of people just get married because they're tired of dating. True love doesn't or hasn't really existed."

"Maybe they just fell in love with the wrong people," Dannon insisted.

"Yeah, that's usually the case."

"I think I see your point, though. See...this is why I want to find the woman of my dreams before I ever get married."

"You'll find the woman of your dreams all right. Just keep going to sleep. Keep snoozing, she'll be there."

"You tryin' to tell me the woman of my dreams don't exist?"

"No, she exists, but you'll have to have your eyes wide open to find her. You can't just fantasize about her. Just keep living, Dannon. Just keep living. But remember, there are no perfect people."

As the temperature began dropping, Dannon could feel goosebumps race up and down his arms. He reached for Kirby's watch and said, "We've been in this car for over an hour. Why don't you come upstairs? Come on, please?"

After another mild protest, Kirby gave in.

THREE

Outwardly, Kirby fronted the nerves of steel; Dannon was with him. Inwardly, he felt uneasy, troubled, angry, and confused. The moment he stepped into the building, memories of his past began to vex him. With the thought of not being at the house he knew as his second home in over eleven years, his heart started to race rapidly and he nearly made a beeline for his car.

"How does it smell?" Dannon teased as they stepped into the elevator.

"All too familiar."

Dannon amusingly took a whiff of the urine-filled odor and said, "You kinda get used to it."

"Will you just press the button?"

Once they arrived Dannon eagerly unlocked the door. "Wait here, Kirby," he said before limping off to the back room. "Momma! You home? I have a surprise for you."

Kirby sat in the trophy-occupied livingroom that

He Was My Hero, Too

once doubled as Bennett's bedroom. A lot had changed in the apartment since his last visit.

Now it was laden with a new matching leather sofa and love seat. There were two glass end tables with lamps on them and a coffee table that had an Oriental rug under it. And the wall was decorated with African paintings.

Kirby spotted a photo album on the coffee table. But what stuck out to him was a picture of the 1973 Mount Vernon High School basketball team. That team led by Bennett, captured Mount Vernon's first and only New York state championship.

The kitchen was equipped with a brand new stove and refrigerator—provided by housing. The beautiful brown eating table, that served as the centerpiece of the dining area, was adorned with tasteful floral place mats and a bowl of plastic fruit.

I wonder where those guys are now? Kirby thought, tracing the image of his former teammates. He knew the fate of his beloved best friend and he knew of himself—the guy who told jokes while riding the bench. Big Joe Hancock, the starting center, went on to play college ball in Florida and got drafted by the Boston Celtics. His brief NBA career ended when he was cut during training camp after pulling a hamstring. Thus, he would opt to play professional ball in Italy—for big bucks. Dexter Stratton, the Bennett clone only 4 inches shorter, attended Iona College, the school Bennett was going to attend, received his degree in English and is now teaching at Mount Vernon High School. Dexter, who still keeps in touch with Kirby on a daily basis, married his college sweetheart and has one daughter. Ronnie O'Koren graduated high school and became part owner of a gas station. Davey "Honey Jack" Sanchez moved to California and didn't leave a contact number. John "Great White Hope" Berry took over his parent's bakery after a dishonorable discharge from the army. Jeffrey Bryce Frazier got strung out on heroin after returning from Vietnam and walks around all day dribbling and shooting an invisible basketball. Brandon "Petty Cash" Jones was killed in Vietnam. Stanley "K" Rowinsky, the guy whose legs formed the letter K whenever he stood still, isn't doing much with his life these days. He's divorced, unemployed, and has three kids. He just lives every day as it comes. Jeffrey Kendall became a background singer for television commercials. And Hezekiah followed in his father's footsteps after graduating theologian school and became a preacher. The "Rev-Doc", as he was now called, became a pastor of Metropolitan Baptist Church, in New Rochelle.

"Kirby", Dannon interrupted Kirby's thoughts. "Momma will be out in a minute."

"Was she asleep? Did you wake her up?"

"You trying to get me killed? She hasn't seen you in years. You haven't been here since Bennett was killed. And you think..."

Kirby held up his hand, "I understand."

He Was My Hero, Too

"Thank you."

As Kirby looked through the photo album, he came across a picture of Bennett holding baby Dannon.

"Do you ever feel pressure being Bennett's younger brother?"

Dannon pondered the inquisition, smiled, and then added, "yeah, sometimes. But, it's a good kind of pressure, more of a pathway. I think if he were alive, I'd still feel, 'the pressure' but now I kind of feel like he's just watchin' over his baby brother and I'm comfortable with it. I wish he were still here, though. I miss my big brother a lot."

"I know the feeling all too well."

"To make me feel better, Momma used to tell me about the story in II Kings in the Bible about Elisha and Elijah. How when Elijah went away to Heaven, he really didn't taste death, he just went up in a flaming chariot, and afterwards, Elisha took over for him. Elisha used to be just like I was with Bennett, always following Elijah around. I kinda feel the same way too. Like Bennett's not really dead, just in Heaven resting or something."

"Your Momma and the Bible."

"Ain't she a trip, though? I mean she has a G.E.D. but, with what, an eighth or ninth grade education? She's probably read every book published. And the woman knows the "Good Book" like the back of her hand."

"That's what you call, 'mother-wit', Dannon."

"Mother what?"

"Kirby, my sweetie." Mrs. Wilson said as she entered

the room wearing a blue flannel nightgown. She hadn't changed much since Kirby last saw her. She still wore a chubby build and a rich head of gray hair. The high blood pressure, which once troubled her, flared up only occasionally. Now that she works in City Hall in the mayor's office, she's able to work day hours instead of a hectic night shift standing on her feet in a factory.

"Mrs. Wilson."

"Well, how've you been? Come here and give me a hug, Son."

"I've been doing fine. It's good to see you," Kirby said during the clinch.

"You look just wonderful. How are Kathy and the boys? Would you like somethin' to eat?"

"No, thank you and everybody is doing fine. And yourself?"

"Oh, Momma's doin' just fine. You know, I'm workin' with the mayor now."

"So I've heard," Kirby said as he pulled away and sat back down. "Mrs. Wilson, I don't mean to be disrespectful or to pry into your business, but I can't stand the guy. I really dislike him a lot. How could you work for him?"

"Momma," Dannon interrupted. "I'm goin' in my room to soak my foot and do my homework. Kirby, I'll see you at the club."

Mrs. Wilson sat beside Kirby and placed her hand on his. "You'll have to find a way to get over it."

"But, he married Tara."

He Was My Hero, Too

"Son, Bennett is gone. Tara is free to marry whomever she pleases."

Reasoning with it, Kirby reluctantly lamented, "Yeah, I guess you're right, but, I just don't like it. She should've married Bennett, that's all."

"I know how you feel. But don't hold grudges, Baby. It's ungodly."

"Mrs. Wilson, I still don't like him. But, I may have to enlist his help in finding Bennett's killer."

"What you say, Kirby?"

"Oh, I'm sorry, Mrs. Wilson."

"What's going on?"

"Mrs. Wilson, I want to find Bennett's killer. It's been twelve years and no one, I mean no one, has been brought to justice. I don't get it."

"I was angered, bitter, and confused myself, but I put it all in God's hand. And I'm really trying to let go. Whoever killed my baby will have their debt to pay sooner or later."

"I know, but—"

"Listen, Kirby, when I lost Bennett, I lost my life. He was my first-born. I cried something terrible, and I seriously thought I was gonna die. Kirby, I never would've thought I'd have to bury my own son. It's a dreadful experience for a parent to bury a child. But, I knew I had to find the strength to go on for Yvette and Dannon's sake. I, on a many days and nights, prayed and asked God to heal my pain."

"Mrs. Wilson..."

"You know something," Mrs. Wilson said while grabbing Bennett's graduation picture off of the end table. "Lord, Bennett gave me the hardest time. I was in so much pain giving birth to that boy. But once I saw him in that incubator, I just knew in my heart, he was going to be something special. Sometimes we have to just accept God's will, trust Him, and move on as best we can."

"Simon said the same thing...in a round-about way."

"I miss my boy, Mrs. Wilson, my brother, and I want justice."

"I understand. So what are you gonna do?"

"Well," Kirby contemplated for a moment then answered, "I asked Simon for help with his street contacts. You know, to see what they can come up with. And, I guess I'll go to the police or whomever it takes to get the job done."

"Good luck, Honey. I wish you all the luck in the world, and I will be prayin' for you day and night. But, be careful. Be so very careful. You still have a family to raise and they need you here and healthy."

Kirby got up to shake off the aggravation and to look at the family pictures. Just as he got to the wall unit, he ran across his all-time favorite, the one with him and Bennett.

# # #

JUNE 1973

Kirby pinched the hand of his best friend Bennett,

He Was My Hero, Too

who lay stone still in his hospital bed, hoping by some miracle he would squeeze back. Kirby, in fear, felt his heart flutter as his mind began to race a million miles a minute. He wished he were a doctor, a genie, or some miracle worker able to reverse the hands of time, thus, having the power to change the fate of whatever he pleased.

Kirby's sick nightmare came to pass and he lost total control of his emotions. The deafening sound of the expired life-pack permeated throughout the hospital room. The uncontrollable tears that flowed from his eyes blinded him. All of a sudden, there was a crash and a trampling sound akin to a herd of raging bull growing louder and more resounding. Kirby looked up, as he had laid his head upon Bennett's chest, and noticed Bennett was being 'bum-rushed' by a team of doctors and nurses.

Kirby was pulled up and backed away by the gentle nudging from one of the nurses. His eyes fixed on Bennett whose only bodily function was the reaction to the shock of the defibrillator. Kirby, realizing the end was imminent, made his way over to the priest who stood outside the room with Bible in tow.

"Father," Kirby said through the rush of tears. "Is there anything you can do for my boy?"

The priest, a stumpy fellow with white hair and thick black glasses, peered inside the room and checked on the doctor and nurses working frantically to revive Bennett. Then he placed his hand on Kirby's shoulder, smiled, and offered, "Son, it's in the Lord's hand now. All we can do is hope, pray, and catch faith."

"I don't think I know what that means, Father."

Just as Kirby was about to offer his imploration for more help, the chief physician approached them with a sullen look.

"No!" Kirby shrieked at the top of his lungs.

The handsome doctor who sported a massive mustache and goatee, stood about six-feet tall and had a bald spot which interrupted the flow of light brown hair, looked at the priest and then back to Kirby and shook his head, "I'm sorry."

Kirby exploded and rushed toward Bennett, only to be held back by doctors.

"No! You gotta do somethin'!"

"Young man," the priest grabbed him. "You have to compose yourself. I know you're hurting."

The physician gave Kirby a tap on the shoulder as a show of support and walked off, mentioning that he had to call Bennett's mother.

Kirby took another glance at Bennett who was fully covered with the bed sheet. Upon seeing this, Kirby snapped. He yelled, raced down the corridor, and shot down the stairwell.

He reached the lobby in no time flat and that's where he met up with Big Joe and Dexter.

"Kirby! What's wrong, man?" A frighten Dexter asked.

"It's Bennett, Dex! He's gone, man! Gone! Gone for

good!"

The three companions formed a circle to console and comfort one another.

"I'm gonna get whoever did this," Kirby said trying to get himself together. "I'm gonna make whoever did this pay, and pay dearly. I'm gonna do him!"

"K-K-Kirby...l-l-let th-th-th..."

"I'm not tryin' to hear nothin' you have to say, Joe, about lettin' the law handle it. Look at how long it's been already. It's been weeks! I'm gonna do it my way. Are you guys with me or what?"

A peep could not be heard from either man, only a look of bewilderment and distress.

"We have to be strong for Bennett's family," Dexter said. "But, you especially."

"Don't tell me what I gotta be, Dex!" Kirby said as he pointed his finger in Dexter's face. "I've been comin' here non-stop for six-weeks. Don't tell me nothin' about bein' strong. Where were you? Huh? Huh?"

"Kirby, what's wrong with you?" Dexter asked.

"Ye-ye-yeah...wh-wh-what's th-th-the matter?" Big Joe also asked.

Kirby served his two friends an expression of disgust before he stormed off lamenting, "I'll handle this my own way! I'll do it myself! I don't need any fair-weather friend no way!"

"Kirby," Dexter chased after him only to get caught and held back by Big Joe.

"Le-le-let him g-g-go, he'll b-b-be fine af-af-after

'while."

As Kirby stormed down the sunny streets of Mount Vernon, he wore a look of rage and confusion. His best friend, his buddy, was gone, shot to death like an animal for no reason. So many unanswered questions traveled in and out of his head: Why couldn't the police find who did it? Why would someone set out to kill Bennett? Why would someone just shoot him in the open—broad daylight—with so many people around? Why would someone shoot him at all?

He decided to break the news to Tara. He reached her house and composed himself by taking in a few deep breaths before ringing the doorbell.

Mister Copeland, Tara's father, answered it and greeted Kirby with his usual, "What's up, Slick?" Kirby exchanged greetings and made his way through the foyer and into the living room and took his seat directly across from Mrs. Copeland. Once eye contact was made, the story was told as Kirby dropped his head in anguish and began to burst into tears.

Mrs. Copeland uttered, "Dear Lord", and proceeded upstairs to get Tara. When Tara entered, she and Kirby embraced.

"Tara," Kirby said while reinforcing his grip around her waist. "He's gone, Tara. He's gone."

"It's going to be all right, Kirby. Everything will be all right. We have to hold on. We're going to have to be strong." Tara broke away and took a seat on the couch to collect her thoughts. "Kirby, we have to be strong for everybody, including ourselves."

Kirby took a seat beside her, "I know Tara, but I have so much anger inside of me. I can't understand this; I can't at all. I don't know what to think and with no arrest or anything."

Tara sucked in a deep breath and released it slowly. "I know and I don't understand that either. But, this is where our faith in the justice system as well as our faith in God must come in."

"I'm sorry, Tara, but when it comes to religion, you know I'm not the most..."

"Well, you have to dig deep for some inner peace now, or..."

Kirby got up, began to pace the room, and then grabbed for the glass of tea Mrs. Copeland had brought him. "I'm going to kill whoever did this!"

"Kirby, please, for goodness, sake, don't start talking like that. It's insane! You'll go to jail!"

"Why do you think I'd get caught?" Kirby said matter-of-factly. "They didn't catch the person who shot Bennett. I probably have more suspects than they do."

"Kirby you can get yourself killed. Do you honestly think Bennett would want that? Please let the police handle it."

Just as Kirby was about to react with more frustration, Tara's parents entered the room. Mr. Copeland sat next to Tara and placed his arm around her, while Mrs. Copeland stood by Kirby and gently rubbed his back.

"Well," Mrs. Copeland said. "I've just spoken with

Mrs. Wilson."

"How is she?" Tara's interest peaked. "I have to get over there."

"She's okay," Mrs. Copeland answered and took a seat. "She's home with Kirby's mother."

"Good, she's not alone."

"She just wants us to pray for her and the rest of the family."

"Mrs. Copeland," Kirby said with a bit of annoyance in his voice. "I don't mind all the prayin' and stuff. But, shouldn't somebody or we be out lookin' for the punk or punks who shot Bennett in the first place? I mean..."

"Son," Mrs. Copeland countered. "In a trying time like this—a tragedy—now is not the time. We in this family are firm believers that prayer changes things. And the Wilson family and friends, especially you, need all the prayers we can get."

FOUR

It was a sweltering summer day with temperatures hovering around the century mark. The date was June 18, 1973. The day the city of Mount Vernon said, "Good-bye", to one of its most honorable sons. Hundreds of family members and friends jammed into Macedonian Baptist Church, the red brick two-story church set in the middle of Ninth Avenue between Second and Third Street.

While scores of despondent family members and friends were inside, what seemed like thousands of well-wishers lined the streets around the church to pay their last respects to the young basketball legend. Bennett would lie in an open oversized brown casket to accommodate his masculine six-foot six-inch frame, dressed in his basketball uniform, amid flowers and a memorial from classmates. His mother sat next to him clutching a photo of him as a baby.

The pastor—Reverend Henry Ewault—was kind enough, at the family's request to have speakers on the outside for those who could not get in. It seemed as though the whole city was there in full-force. The media coverage was enormous. Every newspaper within the tri-state area was there. Television camera crews were set up both inside and outside the church.

Many of the so-called, important, people took their turns paying tribute. Even the governor sent condolences by way of telegram.

The service was so emotionally charged that whenever a well-wisher left the podium after speaking or singing a song, they either left filled with the spirit of the Holy Ghost or in tears.

One song, "Sooner We'll Be Done With the Trouble of This World", sung by Sister Lisa Jackson-Stone, tore into the hearts of many.

Newly appointed principal, Mildred Cummings, of Mount Vernon High was one of the first to speak. Principal Cummings, as she fancied herself to be called, was a slender woman and very elegant. She always wore these big loop earrings and a powerful fragrance of perfume.

She gave a riveting speech that really struck a cord in everyone. But, it was what she said towards the end that made everyone want to check him or herself.

"Some of us, if not all of us, may ask, 'Why did this happen? Bennett was only eighteen years old and such a nice sweet young man. Why did he die?' But the real question we should ask ourselves is, 'Why did he live?'" She paused an instant and looked over the congregation. "Folks, your answer is right in front of you. Your answer is right beside you. Your answer is right behind you. Look at us, we are a mass of humanity sitting sorrowfully but sitting at peace. We are comforting one another; we are supporting one another. But most of all, as a bouquet of different genders, cultures, races and religions, we are finding and showing love for one another. This is a celebration of humanity." She paused, then smiled at the body, "Bennett, my friend, you brought us all together in a very special way. Sure, today we come in sadness, as we should. But today we also come to honor you. Thank you for bringing us together."

Principal Cummings received a loud response of "Amen," from those who agreed with her. "And we should all search inside of ourselves to see if we can challenge ourselves to be able to sustain this love we have shown for one another in this trying time. An incredible war just ended not very long ago. People died over there in Vietnam unnecessarily. But there's still a war going on right over here on American soil. It's called racism. And it's alive and well on almost every turn. Let us pray and try to put an end to all of this madness; let us do it, one and all. I'm not saying give up your cultures. But, let's see if we cán come together as a people. One people. Let's celebrate humanity. Bennett," she said and turned to the casket a second time. "Thank you for giving voice to the concerns which face our youth. You know, dear hearts, this young man was totally against drugs; he was totally against succumbing to peer pressure. He wanted young people to live life to the fullest. He was very much for education and liberation. He was but eighteen years old, this young man. But he was on our side. He was on our side. Oh, Bennett...dear, dear Bennett, sleep on and take your rest. We loved you dearly, but our Creator in Heaven loved you best."

Everyone stood in unison and pounded their hands together. The ovation lasted for nearly two minutes. And that included the folks on the outside. Later, she told the reverend she had not planned to speak so long, but something seemed to grab a hold of her tongue and she could not stop. It was as if a spirit—a pleasant and comforting spirit—were urging her to testify on Bennett's behalf.

When the Reverend Ewault, who was a bronze colored, stout man with a full dark beard that matched the little hair he had left on his head, got up to do the eulogy, he sang a song, "'Till We Meet Again." He then started to reflect on Bennett's time with him.

He reiterated that he knew God's will had and must be done, but from a personal perspective, he grieved. He was able to say, "Bennett, I know that you are in a better place. I just feel that in my heart. Your friends, family, and loved ones, we'll all miss you. You left us too soon. We wish you could've given us just a little more time to love you. But, we thank you for coming into our lives."

He Was My Hero, Too

Kirby sat next to his mother, Lois, on the second pew with the rest of the Wilson family and received their comfort. Bennett's family members consisted of his mother, sister Yvette, brother Dannon, Tara who sat between her parents, and his Aunt Traci.

Albeit a sad day, all went exceptionally well, until it was time to view the body. Suddenly a loud outburst shook the congregation up.

"Get away from me! I'm trying to get to the body!" An enraged man shouted. He was dressed in a wrinkled black suit, dirty white shirt, and ruffled black tie. He also wore a wide-brimmed hat that covered most of his forehead. His walk was very unsteady, which would explain why his shoes were so run over. "I want to see who killed him! I want justice!" He continued wobbling down the middle aisle toward the casket.

"Mister, please," said a male usher who winced and turned his head to fight off the horrible smell. "This is a funeral, have some respect. You can't just come down the aisle like that. If you want to view the body, you'll get your chance, just like everyone else. Please wait your turn."

The man in a snit snatched away from the usher and said, "Move outta my way, boy. Who killed him? Who shot him?"

"Ushers! Ushers!" Reverend Ewault shouted.

"Betty," the man said to Mrs. Wilson as he approached her and removed his hat to fully reveal himself. "Who killed our son? Who shot our boy?"

Mrs. Wilson was overcome with shock she fainted and had to be carried out. The commotion unfortunately did not stop there. Traci, known to have a pretty bad temper, showed no signs different. She was a heavy-set woman with jet-black hair that ran smoothly down her shoulders and she possessed very large hands, which made for cast iron fists when closed. Once Traci gathered herself after being stunned—like the rest of the family—she uncorked a punch to the side of the head of the man that would be Bennett's father. The man who vanished without a trace five years ago would lie lifelessly in a comatose state.

FIVE

OCTOBER 1984

Kirby reversed to make eye contact with a grim-faced Mrs. Wilson who was sitting on the couch.

"I think I'll be heading home now," Kirby said. "I have an early day tomorrow. Man, my head is killing me."

Mrs. Wilson got up and put her hands on Kirby's shoulders. "Don't stay away so long. I know you see Dannon at the Boy's Club, but Momma wants to see you sometimes."

"I'll try, Mrs. Wilson. I'll try."

"Listen, you are gonna have to find a way to get over your pain. Find a way and go on."

"Mrs. Wilson, the only way I'll probably get over this bitterness is when the murderer of Bennett is either caught and put in jail or dead and buried."

Taken aback by Kirby's last elucidation, Mrs. Wilson responded, "Kirby, Son, it don't sound at all like you. I can only imagine just how difficult and frustrating it must be. But you'll have to realize things will work out in time. And as I said before, Bennett's killer will have his day before the Lord. You can count on it."

"Not if I get to him first."

"Kirby..."

"I'm sorry, Mrs. Wilson, but I'll have to work on it."

"I'll be praying for you, praying for you and your family."

"Thank you," Kirby said and kissed Mrs. Wilson on the cheek and left the apartment taking one of Bennett's trophies.

# # #

No sooner than the second Kirby put his key in the door, the telephone rang. In the rare case when he felt like talking to no one, he forced himself to answer it.

"Kirby?"

"Hey Simon, what's up?" Kirby said as he popped a pill in his mouth and collapsed into his reclining chair.

Kirby rented a one-bedroom dwelling in the posh section of White Plains that sat 12 miles north of his hometown and is considered the most metropolitan of all the cities in Westchester County.

He had all the modern appliances and conveniences: plush wall-to-wall carpeting, washer and dryer, a frost-free refrigerator and customized ceiling fans in every room. The flat was armed with a garbage disposal and microwave oven. The intercom system was state-of-the-art; you were able to see the caller on a 15-inch monitor that was imbedded in the wall.

"Got news for you. Sort of, anyway."

"Yeah," Kirby said squinting while applying pressure against his head with a warm rag. "What's up?"

"Well, you asked me if I still had contacts, right?"

"Yeah," was Kirby's response again, only this time with more excitement. He began to sit up straight. "Whatcha got?"

"I got a hold of an old buddy of mine, Harry Hooch. He just got out of prison. He may know a few people. He's gonna make a few calls, then get back to me, probably tomorrow or Thursday the latest."

"Man, that's great, fantastic. Where do we go from here?"

Simon, ever the deliberate one these days, cautioned, "Not so fast, let's just wait and see what Hooch has to say. He may have something or he may not have anything at all."

"Let's hope he has plenty."

"I have faith in him, if there's anything out there, he'll find it for us."

"Solid!"

"So, I'll see you and your boys at 'Brotherhood Night', tomorrow, right?"

"I don't know about that one."

"You want help from me, don't you?"

"Aw, Simon, don't go there on me."

"Hey," Simon said affirmatively, "one good turn deserves another. I'll see you tomorrow."

"Yeah, Simon," Kirby blew into the air, "okay."

"Goodnight, my friend. Oh! By the way, I have another..."

"Joke? Simon, do I have to?"

"Yes, just listen. This guy's wife died. And after the funeral, the grief-struck husband rode back in the limo with his best friend. The friend was trying desperately to comfort his sobbing main man. The best friend said, 'Larry, one day, maybe not soon, but not too far off either; this will all pass. No. Not the memory of your wife, your confidant, your lover, your soul mate, but all of this pain. And someday, maybe even sooner than you think, someone else will come along, not to replace your wife, but to fill a part of your life. She'll be more than willing to share that time with you. And one of these days, I promise, you'll find her and you'll have a full and enriching life again. One day, she'll be there.'

Larry stopped crying, looked at his friend, and said, 'Yeah, I understand all that, but...but, what am I gonna do about tonight?"

Simon after an extended crack up called back to Kirby, "How's that? Did you like that one? Kirby? Kirby? Kirbster? Kirb? Kirby?"

SIX

JUNE 1973

"Dust to dust, ashes to ashes," Reverend Ewault said just as he was crushing a flower over Bennett's coffin while the undertakers were laying him down to his eternal rest. Overall, there had to be more than 50 cars that followed the procession from the church in Mount Vernon to the cemetery in Valhalla, NY, some twenty miles away.

To keep the travel flowing smoothly, state troopers closed down the northbound side of Interstate 287.

Bennett's gravesite would be on a hill overlooking a dam of water.

Kirby, who was dressed in a black pinstriped suit, stood along side with the rest of the basketball team. Dannon tugged away at Traci's side, while Yvette tried unsuccessfully to comfort her mother.

Kirby, glancing across to Dexter who was standing beside him wearing a brown suit and dark shades and vowed, "I'm gonna get whoever did this."

"Le-le-let the po-po-police ha-ha-handle it, K-K-Kirby," Big Joe advised.

"He's right, man. Let the police handle it. We're all upset over this, but let them handle it. We keep tellin' you this. Play it safe. Hey, whoever killed Bennett is obviously still out there. He or they must be dangerous. Let the police handle it."

Kirby looked Dexter straight in the eye and deadpanned, "I am the police. I'll find them and bring them into my own justice."

Big Joe who had recently chopped down his bushy Afro and added an extra 10 pounds of muscle, making him a beefed-up six-foot eight and 250 pounds, began to get nervous. As he attempted to speak, he initiated patting his foot and slapping his thigh. Nothing would come out until he was able to settle down, "K-K-Kirby, be careful."

"I will be. I will be."

# # #

"Son, where are you going?" Kirby's mother Lois asked from her seat at the kitchen table. Lois was a young looking forty-something brown-skinned woman. Her face was sprinkled with tiny moles. She was a slender and petite woman. She, like the rest of the females in her family, had hips the size of Texas. It was alleged that once, when Lois was crossing a busy street in downtown New York City, wearing tight blue jeans, she caused a nine-car accident because a driver failed to take his eyes off of her. And guys from the neighborhood would joke with Kirby telling him, "Pam Grier ain't got nothin' on your Moms!"

"I'm going out for a walk. I need some air."

"It's almost midnight and it's raining like crazy out there. Kirby, do we need to talk? Son, you can talk to me. You do know this, don't you?"

"Yes. I know, Momma, I know. But, I just, I just need to get some air. I'll be back shortly, I promise." Kirby said kissing his mother's forehead. "Don't wait up for me, though."

"You bet I'll wait up. Here, take my umbrella."

Seconds later, Kirby was out trekking the darkened and drenched streets of Mount Vernon. He did not know where he was going, but he walked, and walked, and walked.

His travel took him to a place where he came across dope-slinging Simon. Simon was standing outside the Dew Drop Inn bar, with his companion Willie and another man holding a walking cane.

Kirby quickened his pace and purposely brushed against Simon with his shoulder.

"Excuse me, young fella," Simon said after the intentional hit.

"Man, if I find out that you have anything to do with my boy's murder...I promise you! I'll kill you! You understand me?"

Kirby was collared before he could bat an eye.

"Whoa, Willie, he's just a kid, just a kid. Let him go;

it's all right."

"I'll show you how much of a kid I am. I'll shove that umbrella down your throat!"

"You better quit while you're ahead," Willie demanded.

"It's cool, Willie," Simon said flashing a smirk. "Now, now, young fella. First off, I had nothing to do with Bennett's murder. I was out of town on business when it occurred."

"Like you couldn't get somebody to do your dirty work. Like one of your dope fiend flunkies."

"Murder is not my game. Never has been, never will be."

"What do you call that mess you push on the streets?"

"Feel Good," Simon said as he laughed and received a five from Willie.

"I'll show you, Feel Good," Kirby countered and dropped Simon with a right to his jaw.

Willie charged Kirby and lifted him up over his head. Just as he was about to smash him to the pavement, Simon rose to his feet and put his rain-soaked hat back on.

"Let him go, Willie."

"But, Simon, he just..."

"Turn him loose! Now, I said!"

"You're lucky, kid," Willie said to Kirby as he gathered himself and picked up his umbrella.

"This ain't over, Simon! You too, Bubba!"

Simon stood amidst the weighty downpour and watched Kirby as he stormed down the street.

Willie walked over to his boss, handed him a handkerchief, and asked, "You okay? Do you want me to break him up once and for all?"

With his eyes still affixed on Kirby, Simon wiped the blood from his mouth, "No, don't hurt him. As a matter-of-fact, I want you to protect him."

"Say what?"

"You heard me," Simon said as he shoved the bloody handkerchief in Willie's chest. "I want him protected. You guys are responsible for his safety. See to it nothing happens to him."

"Boss," Willie said, "I don't understand."

"There's a thing called friendship. And that kid lost his best friend. He's got a lot of heart. He cared about his boy. That's loyalty. I like that."

"Who do you think could've done it?" asked Little Tiny Smalls, the other man standing with Simon and Willie. Little Tiny Smalls was a huge man; he had to be at least 360 pounds. He had this great big water tank head and the biggest eyes you ever saw. He was a dark complexioned man with colored blond hair. And the cane was not for walking. Tiny Smalls had no limp nor did he have a bad leg. The cane was used in large part to crack heads.

"You got me, Tiny. I didn't hear anything of a contract out on him. Who knows, it could've been out-of-towners."

"But," Willie jumped in. "Who would want to kill a

high school ball player like that? I mean, he was 'Bennett.' How many enemies could he have?"

"Listen," Simon said just as he was about to get into the back seat of his navy blue white-walled Caddie. "I want you to put a tail on him. Nothing obvious. I want a light tail. He just lost his partner. But at the rate he's going, he'll be joining him. Don't let anything happen."

"I'll get right on it," Tiny Smalls said. "I'll go inside and make few calls."

# # #

"Kirby, you're soaked," Tara, who was clad in a pink flannel nightgown with matching robe and oversized Bugs Bunny slippers, said upon greeting him. "Whew! You're drunk, too. Come on inside, it's pouring out."

Tara, who was also grieving and a bit confused herself, managed to keep her 'runway model' looks intact.

"I know it's late, but I need to talk to someone," Kirby said as he staggered inside. Tara's family had the biggest and prettiest house on the block, but they were constantly changing the color of it. Whatever the mood was for Tara's father, that's the color he chose. The outside was painted lavender trimmed in purple.

"Sure, it's not a problem. I understand."

"You weren't asleep, were you?"

"No," Tara said and took Kirby's unopened umbrella away from him. "I was just sitting here with Sol discussing plans for college."

"Sol? What's he doin' here?"

He Was My Hero, Too

"Kirby?"

"Where is he?" Kirby said and stormed passed her.

Sol overheard the commotion and sat nervously at the dining room table in front of a cup of hot chocolate.

"Kirby, come here!"

Kirby snatched Sol's hat and raincoat and mashed them against his sternum.

"Tara, what's up?"

"Hey man, what are you doin' here this time of night? Bennett just died. What's up with this?"

As Sol began to express, "You wouldn't hit a guy with glasses on, would you?" Kirby had taken two swings at him. The first one missed and missed badly. The second one seemed to come from South America and knocked him silly, on the word, *you*.

By instinct, Sol immediately began searching for his glasses while scrambling to get to his feet. He managed to tell Tara, "I'll see you some other time. I'm out of here!"

Kirby went after him again, but Tara moved quickly, and pushed him back, "Kirby, are you crazy? What's wrong with you?"

"Honey," Tara's mother said from the top of the steps. "What's going on down there? Is everything all right?"

"Yes, Ma. Kirby's here, he just slipped and fell."

"Is he, okay?" Mrs. Copeland asked as she started making her way down the long spiral steps.

"Hi, Mrs. Copeland," Kirby said as he turned his face to shield the odor of alcohol fuming from his mouth.

"I'm fine, thanks."

"Well, be careful now," Mrs. Copeland admonished after making sure everything was fine. "Okay, kids, I'm going back to bed."

"Goodnight, Ma."

Kirby and Tara then sat on the couch and proceeded to talk in a quiet chatter.

"Kirby," Tara said as he arose from the couch with her arms flailing in the air. "You have to go on with your life."

"Tara, what are you talkin' about?"

"I'm going to go on with mine. I have no other choice." Tara took her seat again next to Kirby. "Bennett," she said as tears began to well up in her eyes, "he wasn't the first boyfriend I lost. My first boyfriend—we were both in the seventh grade, he died of leukemia. We had been dating for nine months, almost about the same amount of time as Bennett and I."

"Tara, I'm sorry. I really am, but..."

"Kirby," Tara arose from her seat once again, this time with more fury. "No! We have to move on!"

"He was my boy!"

"Well, he was my man!"

After making eye contact, they realized things weren't going too well, so Tara, in earnest, switched the subject. "I'll be leaving for school soon. Kirby, stay positive. Kathy tells me you've been acting a little strange lately. She says you've been hanging out a lot, and she thinks you've been drinking a lot."

He Was My Hero, Too

"Oh, she does, does she?"

"Well," Tara said a bit more annoyed. "I know you've been drinking. I can smell it on your breath a mile away."

"I don't need this," Kirby said as he lifted himself off of the couch and headed for the door.

"Kirby," Tara said and grabbed him by the arm. "You better get it together. We just got out of a war. And all they need to see is you milling around the streets doing nothing and they…"

"Tara," Kirby said as he yanked himself away from her. "You have a good night."

Kirby took to the streets again. He was so intense, since he left out of a liquor store—a second time in the same night—he failed to notice the heavy downpour had pretty much stopped. In the act of treading past his building in a trance, he boarded a bus. He took a seat in the back. He was alone, except for two other passengers seated in the middle.

His world was spinning like a top, and there was no concept of time.

"Whoa! Whoa! Bus man," Kirby called out to the driver, the only other person on the bus. "This is my stop!"

Kirby got up slowly and relocated towards the rear door.

"Young man," the salt and pepper haired bus driver said. "This is a cemetery. This isn't a regular stop at this hour…"

Kirby made his way about the front-end of the bus next to the driver. "Mister, let me off of this bus."

"Young man..."

Kirby began to get agitated with the driver as his facial expression changed, "You better let me off this bus, if you know what's good for you."

"Young man, I have a wife and three children at home. I don't want any trouble."

"Good," Kirby said, still slightly inebriated. "Because, you see these, I've already knocked two people out tonight."

"You win," the driver said as he pulled over on the pitch-dark road. "Here's your stop. Have a good evening."

"I thought you might see it my way. Good evening to you, too," Kirby said and staggered off the bus with package in tow.

Kirby walked around in circles for several minutes before he reached a second cemetery entrance gate. With very little hesitation, he flung the package over the fence and into a bushy area.

"Ruff! Ruff! Ruff!" He barked as he looked for another living creature, on two or four legs. When there was no response, Kirby looked around, and with the agility of an alley cat, he skillfully scaled the six-foot fence.

Kirby was able to recover his package with the aid of his flashlight. He then preceded walking, searching tombstone by tombstone.

In conclusion, he spotted Bennett's and dropped his package and sat down in a yoga position. He then tore into it and pulled out a bottle of rum.

He Was My Hero, Too

"Bennett," he said taking a swig, "I'm sorry man. You shouldn't be layin' there. I should be there." Kirby wiped away at his face and in the same motion threw his head back to accept another drink. "I mean...this is probably all my fault. I mean, you told me about this dream you had about dyin', and I didn't take you seriously. You even told me on several occasions that you thought someone was followin' you. I didn't listen. I was hardheaded and now look at what happened. You get shot right before my very eyes." Kirby mumbles, moans and takes another swig. "You had so much talent. You were so gifted with so much to give; so much to live for. I thought you'd be here forever." Kirby belches then swallows more rum. "Now, look at me. I have no talent, no hope, no desire, no nothin'. You tell me, Bennett, who should be here, me or you?"

Kirby went into his bag once more and this time he pulled out a needle and a syringe. But just as he was about to stick himself, a voice from nowhere called out to him, *Don't do it. Don't do it to yourself. Kirby, you have so much to live for. You have something to live for. You have so much to live for...so much to live for.*

A frightened and troubled Kirby shot back, "Who's there?"

Don't destroy yourself, Kirby. You have your whole life ahead of you. I love you, Kirby. Don't destroy yourself. Live! Live! Live! Live!

"Bennett, is that you?"

Suddenly a beam of light jolted Kirby back. It was a

light so intense he had to squint his eyes and fend off with his hands.

"Young man," came a voice resonating from a huge figure hanging in what appeared to be a raincoat. "What are you doing here?" The voice was followed by a growl, which belonged to an enormous German shepherd.

"Hey Mister, hold your dog! Hold your dog back!"

"Don't worry about him, you just get out of here before I call the police."

"Go ahead and call them. I could use the free ride home anyway."

"What's in your hand?"

"What? This?" Kirby said piercing at the bottle. "This is apple juice."

"That's not apple juice."

"It's apple juice."

"That's not apple juice."

"It's apple juice."

"That's not apple juice, youngman," the man said with more force as he tugged on his dog. "Matter-of-fact, I've been noticing those bottles around here lately when I do my rounds in the mornings. Have you been sleeping out here?"

"Do I look like a bum to you, Mister? Hey! Call your dog back!"

"Are you gonna leave now, or do I have to call the police?"

"I'm going, Mister, I'm going."

The man yanked his dog back again. Fortunately, Kirby would not be his late-night snack.

SEVEN

OCTOBER 1984

"It's Wednesday night!" Simon said into the microphone. "Do you guys know what night it is?"

"It's Brotherhood Night!" The voices rang from the bleachers of the South Side Mount Vernon Boy's and Girl's Club. The club was located on the corner of Sixth Avenue and Fifth Street. In fact, its gymnasium took up the entire corner block of Fifth Avenue. The outside of the club was coated with bright yellow paint. The basketball court was usually lit with the skylights during the day. Whereas the club did have lights, they were normally dim. The floor was a marble caramel brown tile. And the dark brown bleacher seats accommodated anywhere from 1,500 to 2,000 bodies.

Simon did a double take when he spotted Kirby standing by the entrance with his two sons.

"You made it," Simon said as he approached them.

The crowd of young men and fathers were singing and clapping to the music that whisked from the public address system.

"Man," Simon said as he hugged Kirby, "I'm awfully glad to see you. I thought you weren't gonna show."

"Kathy and I had to get the boys new sneakers. I told you, I'd be here."

"Ah, hah. Did I hear a family outing? See I told you, you guys will be all right."

"It's not like that, we always get the boys clothes together."

"Hey, by the way," Simon remembered. "Why'd you hang up on me last night?"

"Man, I didn't hang up," Kirby said and laughed. "I fell asleep. You need to shorten those long and drawn-out jokes of yours."

"Well," Simon said and walked off, laughing, "I saved you a seat on the dais."

Kirby sent his boys to the bleachers and took a seat along side Boy's Club officials, Lowes Moore and James Jones.

The podium was a makeshift chair and table ensemble, five chairs and one long table set in the middle of the gymnasium floor.

Simon, dressed in a navy blue business suit, white shirt and paisley tie, made his way back to the microphone. He stood in silence absorbing the invaluable moment. Simon looked around and noticed the many new faces in the crowd. He then focused on the banners that hung from the rafters: "NEW RO IS IN THE HOUSE ", "TUCKAHOE, ALWAYS ON THE GO", "PELHAM, PELHAM, JUST HERE TO TELL."

He Was My Hero, Too

The presence of Black, White, Hispanic, Asian and American Indians intensely moved Simon. The smorgasbord of humanity netted also the likes of gang-bangers from rival gangs, would-be gang-bangers, drug dealers, drug addicts, pimps, professionals, school kids as well as scholars. The Nation of Islam provided security, so there was no need to feel uncomfortable. Simon detested that people had to be governed but rationalized it was for the best. Kirby, for one, was somewhat taken aback by the masses which ranged in age from eight years-old to senior citizens. The crowd spilled out onto the floor, and up and down both baselines.

At the start of Simon's lectures, he would request all those seated in groups to disburse. He wanted everyone to sit next to someone they did not know. He encouraged peace and comfort among those not of themselves.

Simon's mind went adrift to when he was in prison. One night while laying face down and in a deep sleep alone in his cell, Simon felt a poke to his back.

"Wake up! Wake up, I said Simon!"

Simon thought it was a guard doing a routine bed check and offered sheepishly, "What is it? What do you want? Go bother somebody else and leave me alone."

"Wake up, Simon!" The voice and poke came again. Only this time the voice was louder and the poke was much harder.

"Man, it's early. I'm going back to sleep. Good night."

"Wake up, Simon! Now!" The voice ordered yet again. This time with even more force. Simon still elected to ignore the orders. That was until he felt a smack to his back that felt as if it came from a baseball bat. Simon in haste turned over and was blinded by a bright light. Simon's fears became even more intense when he realized the light was not from a prison guard's flashlight. The light appearing before him seemed to be every bit of nine-feet tall and three-feet wide.

"What's going on?" Simon asked with fear and trembling. "Are you here to kill me?"

"Simon!" The voice cried out. "You have blood on your hands!"

Simon cowering tried to duck his head under a core of blankets. It was to no avail. The strong and cold wind that whisked across the cell nearly decapitated him.

"I'm sorry. I'm so sorry for what I've done."

"You have a debt to pay, Simon."

"I'll do anything. Anything. Please, don't kill me. I'll do whatever you ask."

"Save the lives that you've lost. Save the lives that you've lost! You have blood on your hands!"

"How do I do that?" Simon said still trembling as he heard the sounds of babies crying. The voices then stopped and gave way to the sound of gunshots.

"You owe, Simon! You owe!"

# # #

Within minutes, the musical chairs had stopped, and

He Was My Hero, Too

everyone was settled again. This time when Simon approached the microphone, the ovation was louder and stronger.

"Please take the hand of your neighbor and then let's bow our heads in a moment of silence, in respect for those who have fallen needlessly to gang violence. As Simon bowed his head, he hoped others would pray in silence, as he did.

"Peace to all of you."

"Peace to you too, Bra Simon," the mass of humanity roared back. Simon took pride in his ability to say the word "peace" in several different languages.

"Thank you. And it's so good to see you all. I won't be too long."

"Take your time, Bra Simon! This is your night!" A voice came from the audience.

"No, we have school children here, and I want to be mindful. Anyway, I'm gonna get right to it. I'm appealing to you young men and some of you young women." Simon stopped for a moment and smiled. "Yeah, I see you've infiltrated the ranks. It's okay for now; you're most welcomed. But, on a serious note, we must stop the killing. You gang-bangers, pushers, dealers, stop the madness. These guns...hey, if you guys want to shoot something, shoot basketballs. Not guns! Some of you guys have been doing a good job, a great job with the Midnight Hoops here at the club. You must continue it. Shoot hoops, not guns. You guys doing these drugs, you guys are killing yourselves, your communities and your families. Fellas, look at the big picture. Really. What good is it to gain the whole world and lose your soul and kill off a brother or sister in the process? It really isn't worth it. And yes, I'm speaking from experience. I've been there. I was a menace to society just like some of you. I sold dope, I hooked women, and I ran numbers. But, it took me going to prison for the light to get turned on again. And I said "again" because you people are looking at a man with a masters degree in psychology."

Simon saw there were murmurs throughout the crowd, came back again, "Yes, I said a masters degree. I lost my way for a time, but through the help of God and through my lovely wife, I was able to come back. You may not get the same privilege as I did. You might die before it's too late. I can't tell you guys how to serve God. That's your natural right under the United States Constitution. But, by and large...educate yourselves! Read books! Learn more about life. You guys that are in schools, stay there for the duration. Complete the necessary requirements in order that you get that piece of paper. People, education is the key that unlocks the door to so many opportunities; take full advantage of that. I want you people to know something. I had an opportunity to earn thousands of dollars on the lecture circuit. But, I forfeited the opportunity. Why? It's because I love you. And I want to see each and every one of you make it. I don't want to see you, especially those of you that are so-called 'at risk', to go out like

He Was My Hero, Too

that. I want to see you go far in this life and be the men you can become. I want to see you men and women living at peace with one another. Yes, Black, White, Hispanic, Asian, Indian, American-Indian, Jew, rich man or poor man; let's all live in peace and harmony."

Simon stepped away from the podium and received a thunderous round of applause. "And one more thing I want to add in my closing remarks. I want you guys to stand. No, not physically stand, but spiritually stand! Make a stand! Take a stand! And stand for something right! Something positive! Something true! Because if you don't, you'll fall for anything!"

Simon concluded by raising his hand in a peace gesture as the crowd rose to its feet and showered him with cheers, whistles and a continuous round of hand clapping.

As always, Simon would ask, "You guys ready for this one?"

"Yes!" Came the jubilant response.

"Okay, well here goes. Agnes, a local socialite, was having this gathering, a tea party of sorts, for the ladies cultural club. Agnes spent days on end preparing for this gala event. And all was going well, that is, until little Abner, her 4-year-old son, came a running in and yelling, 'Mummie! Mummie! Mummie! I think I gotta make a pee-pee.' Embarrassed and humiliated, Agnes ushered little Abner upstairs and gave him a tongue lashing, 'Son, the next time you have to make a pee-pee, don't yell, just come to me and tell me that you have to whisper.' Little Abner took the scolding to heart and went back out to play.

That night after everyone was asleep, little Abner awoke and went into his parent's bedroom. He started jumping up and down and tugged on his daddy's nightshirt. And sleepily, his daddy woke up, 'What do you want, little Abner?' Big Abner asked. 'I gotta whisper, Daddy. I gotta whisper really bad.' 'Whisper? Surely, son, surely.' Big Abner said and leaned his head over the side of the bed. 'Just, whisper right here in my ear.'"

The seriousness and melancholy of the moment capriciously changed to mass hysteria. Simon found himself in stitches as he laughed all the way back to his office.

"Bra Simon, can I speak to you a minute?"

"Sure, Ricky, come on in. Have a seat." Ricky Gates was one of the fellas from the neighborhood. Ricky, in his mid-twenties, was part of a large family, which was made up of six brothers and seven sisters. Ricky's family—brothers and sisters—had a strange similarity; they all had lazy left eyes.

"What can I do for you?"

"Yeah, Bra Simon, I want to tell you your speech really moved me. I mean really, really moved me. I mean really..."

"Thank you, Ricky. Now what's up?"

"Oh yeah, yeah...well as I was sitting there listened to you speak..."

"'Listened' to me speak?"

"Sorry, I meant, 'listening to you speak,' I was saying

He Was My Hero, Too

to myself, 'how can I or what can I do myself to contribute to this situation? You know, help out some."

"Of course."

"Well here goes...I started to write this poem, you see. A little somethin' to represent the sista's."

"You have it there? Let's hear it."

"Check it out, check it out, check this thing out."

"I'm checking, I'm checking, I'm checking already."

"Here's the title, 'DA FREAKS WIT DA BIG ONIONS'!"

Simon crossed his eyes, sat and slid back in his chair, "Whoa! Whoa! Whoa! What?"

"DA FREAKS WIT DA BIG ONIONS. You know, it's about those girlies with the...Pow! Pow! Big—"

"Ricky," Simon pointed toward the door. "Get outta my office! Get out, now! If you want to stay for midnight basketball, feel free, but in the mean time, get out. Read a book or something. Go to one of the reading workshops. But, don't take that with you. Please don't."

"Aw, Bra Simon, this is just my creative genius. My way of sayin'..."

"Good-bye Ricky."

"I'm out. Oh, hey Kirby, how you doin'?"

"I'm cool," Kirby said and held the door for the departing poet. "Simon, was that Ricky Gates?"

"Yeah, that's him," Simon said shaking his head in disbelief.

"His mind is bad, ain't it?"

"Yeah. But, I think something is wrong with the

whole family. If you ask me, I think somewhere down the line some of his relatives married each other."

Kirby closed the door and took the seat Ricky had just occupied. "They can't be that bad. Can they?"

"Da freaks with the big onions."

"What did you say? Simon, you still trying to tell those corny jokes?"

"What corny jokes, chump? Where's your sense of humor?"

"Humor? Where's my sense of humor? Where's your sense of dignity?"

Simon leaped from his chair and hopped across his desk, knocking over a paper bin in the process.

"Chump," Simon said and fixed himself into a boxing stance. "I'll show you 'chump.' Put 'em up."

Kirby rose from his seat and joined Simon in the imaginary boxing ring.

"Talk is cheap, you know?"

"Oh, so I suppose listening to you is expensive?"

"Old man, you don't want none of this."

"Old?" Simon took a jab at the air, missed by a country mile. "Old, I'll show you old. I ain't lost nothin'."

"Of course," Kirby said and returned an errant jab. "How can you lose something you never had? Ever."

The office door swung open just before *golden gloves* could strain a muscle.

"Is this a private affair or can anyone join?" Jimmy Jones, the head director of the Southside Boys and Girls Club said upon entering. Mr. Jones, along with regional director, Billy Thomas, was the mastermind behind getting Simon to join the staff. They also gave him the idea, citing his personality and gift of gab, of having the Brotherhood Night and Midnight Basketball Tournaments.

"Jim," Kirby said as the two shook hands. "What time is it?"

"10:30."

"Whoa, Kathy's gonna kill me. I better get the boys home; it's past their bedtime. I'll see you cats later."

"Those boys are growing up fast. They're a good size. I could definitely use them on the Junior Sonics. Bring them by on Saturday, if you can."

"Sounds good, but if I can't make it, I'll be sure Kathy brings them. They'll play."

"Good...and tell Kathy, I said hello. And Simon," Jim dressed in a brown three-piece suit said to a pooped out man, "don't forget our board meeting on Friday at 1:00."

"I'll be there, boss. Oh!"

"Something wrong?"

"Oh no, it's just, I promised my daughter, I'd take her to her ballet lesson on Friday. But..."

"What time is her lesson?"

"4:30."

"We should be long finished by then, if not, just leave. It's just a briefing. Don't want you to break any promises."

At the end, Simon had a moment to himself to reminisce on the day's events. He thought of his speech and felt a chill. The response he received was the greatest he ever had, and that includes all the sermons he preached in church.

It was an hour and a half before midnight basketball so he decided he would change into his warm-up gear. As he reached for the door to lock it, he felt a strange tug coming from the other side. Thinking it was jammed, he tugged away at it again, this time with more force. Hence, it opened and whom did he see? Jay Rock, all six-feet five inches of him. Jay Rock who had a nasty scar down the left side of his face, also sported a goatee and his two front teeth were studded with diamonds.

"Can I help you?" Simon asked in surprise at the mass of humanity standing before him.

"Yeah, you can," Jay Rock said and bogarted his way in. Once he was in, he flicked the toothpick that he had hidden in his mouth onto the floor, and motioned to Simon to sit down.

"Look here, Jay Rock," Simon said as he noticed Jay Rock open his vest and flash his six-inch knife. "I'm drenched. I was just about to change my clothes. I'll..."

"This will only take a few, have a seat...Please?" Jay Rock's voice seemed to take on a different tone, a much deeper and deliberate one.

Simon unwillingly accommodated Jay Rock's request, "Okay, I'm sitting. What can I do for you?"

"Well," Jay Rock said and dropped his size 14's on top of Simon's desk. "I gotta give it to you. You definitely have a way with captivatin' people. I mean, the way you can get their attention and keep it for a long period of time. That's a gift."

"Thank you," Simon said and reached across the desk and slapped down the combined twenty-eight.

"I truly appreciate your speeches, like I said. But, the reality is, you're takin' away my business. You're takin' food off my table and I don't like that."

"Say, what?"

"You got customers leavin' me and convertin' to what you're tellin' them. Some of my workers have also gone soft on me."

Simon sat back and felt good about himself. The notion of some of his 'pearls of wisdom' reaching a few made him even more confident.

"I'm sorry, but I can't help you," Simon shot back with a coy smile.

Jay Rock again opened his vest, this time a tad bit wider.

"Man, listen. And get that sappy smile off your face. This is serious business."

"Jay Rock, your Boy Scout knife doesn't scare me. Not one bit. Your size doesn't scare me either. Man, I tossed down guys like you for breakfast in the joint."

"This is Mount Vernon. This ain't no cell block. I ain't one of your little cell mates."

"You don't care about what you're doing to your own people do you? Some people in society just love it when we kill each other. You're feeding right into their hands."

"Yo, Simon, you were just like me, once. And now you're so righteous and so holier-than-thou? You ain't no better than me. I'm survivin'. I'm gettin' mines. And I'll die for mines, to protect mines. That's my word."

"There's always a better way of surviving. Get a job, a real job. Get out there and hustle like everybody else. And the fact that you're willing to die or be killed like a dog in the streets...I don't get it. Do you realize there are a number of businesses in this area alone, who are scared to death when school lets out at 3:00? In fact, some even go so far as to close their stores at that time. They're scared of the children. And what kind of example do you think you're setting? Does it make sense to you, at all?"

"Who cares if it makes sense? It's not my problem or my concern. I have my own dollars to make," Jay Rock again flashed his knife. "Whoever gotta do what they gotta do, don't scare me."

The hostile conversation continued for nearly an hour. That was until Simon's patience ran out.

"Jay Rock, this conversation is over!"

Jay Rock gave Simon a dirty look after he sucked his teeth. "Man, you better watch yourself, and stay out of my business."

"Just get out!" Simon yelled as he opened the door, revealing his wife LoNelle.

"Honey, what's up? Whoa, stop!" LoNelle had to step in front of Simon to keep him from going after Jay Rock.

"Stay away from my kids, Jay Rock! Stay away from my kids!"

# # #

"Kathy," Kirby said and sat down on his couch and

popped a pill. "I have the boys with me. You weren't home, and I didn't want to leave them alone. I'll run them off to school tomorrow. I understand you went to the mall with your mother. That's, fine. But, it was getting late and my head started to hurt. Yes, I am getting it checked out, first chance I get. Woman, please will you stop questioning me! You're stressin' me! Kathy? Kathy? Hello? This woman hung up on me. Well, I'll be..."

"Daddy," Bennie said as he walked into the living room. "Who you talkin' to, Daddy...Mommy?"

Many described Bennie to be as cute as a button. But he neither favored Kirby nor Kathy with his huge dimples that sheltered each cheek and curly dark brown hair that drew up really tight whenever it became wet.

"No son," Kirby said and sat down and held his head. "Is your brother out of the bathroom?"

"Yes."

"Well, you guys get in the bed and I'll be there in a minute to tuck y'all in."

"Okay, Daddy. When are you comin' back home?"

"Uh, I don't know right now."

"I...I mean, we miss you bein' there with us."

"I miss being there with you guys also."

"Daddy, you all right?"

"I'm fine, Bennie. Now go on, get in the bed."

"Why you holdin' your head like that then?"

Kirby picked his head up momentarily to answer, "No reason, Son, now go on." Kirby tapped the backside of the interrogator in the red and blue Superman pajamas.

Eight

JUNE 1973

The sun glistened as brightly as ever on this midsummer's day. Two weeks have passed since Bennett was buried, but that was hardly adequate time for Kirby to get over anything, especially since he was so dissatisfied with the way the police had been mishandling the situation. He felt the police were way off base in the way they went about their investigation. He nearly came to blows with one detective when his own mother was asked to go to the police station for questioning.

In the process of days whisking by, his ever-growing disdain for the city he called home began to mount. Reading the local papers and watching the local news on television became more and more depressing.

Kirby decided he wanted to shoot some hoops at Fourth Street playground, a first since he and Bennett played there several months ago.

He knew the event would be somewhat difficult, and he refused to go through it alone. Kirby called Dexter and Big Joe, to ask them to hang out. They agreed on the condition that Kirby promise to lighten up and allow himself to enjoy the moment. Kirby acquiesced, but crossed his fingers during the pledge.

Following several games of h-o-r-s-e, o-u-t, and twenty-one, along with working on drills, the three amigos decided to listen to the message their bodies were sending, which was to take a rest. Kirby surprisingly sprung for the soft drinks that he purchased from the hot-dog truck stationed just outside the park.

"Thanks, Kirby, that hit the spot," Dexter said as he lay sun-soaked and sprawled across the wooden bleachers.

Big Joe who was on his second 16oz. Pepsi managed to toast the air and nod his head in approval.

"Don't mention it. Besides, I owed you for takin' my spot on the Sonics."

"No problem," Dexter said as beads of sweat poured profusely out of his skin. "I needed the practice time anyway."

"S-s-so d-d-did you m-m-make up your mind about w-w-what you gonna do?"

"Not quite, big fella. I have somethin' in mind, though."

Dexter, who had had enough of being cooked by the sun, decided to sit up. "You're not gonna stay around here and do nothing are you?"

"B-b-but y-y-you," Big Joe said in frustration as he stomped the ground and pounded on the basketball. "Ain't gonna try t-t-to be no detective, are you?"

Kirby held up his hands, "I plead the fifth."

"Let the police handle this, man," Dexter offered.

"The police? Who, Mutt and Jeff?"

"Kirby, I know you may have been closer to Bennett than we were, but we love him just the same. He was our boy too. I don't want you gettin' yourself hurt or killed, Dude."

"Yeah, but do you think Bennett is restin' comfortably in his grave? He's probably turnin' over now, just as we speak, knowin' the person who killed him is still on the loose."

"Kirby..."

"Forget it, Dex," Kirby said and waved his hand at him. "When are you guys leavin' for school?"

"I sh-sh-ship out Au-Au-August 22nd."

"I don't know yet," Dexter said still visibly annoyed. "A teammate of mine is supposed to call me to let me know when the apartment will be ready. But my guess would be mid to late August, like Big Joe."

"Well, I hope you both make it to the NBA. I could sure use those free tickets to Knicks' games. Either that or sell them for some moolah."

"I knew there was a catch to those sodas," Dexter said to Big Joe and the two slapped five.

"Very funny," Kirby playfully shoved Dexter.

Kirby, for no apparent reason glanced over his shoulder as two of his favorite little people entered the park, "Yvette...and Dannon!" Kirby called in their direction.

Dannon located the voice and ran towards him as fast

He Was My Hero, Too

as his little legs would carry.

"Kirby!" Dannon said as he jumped into his arms. Kirby proudly held him tight and kissed him on the back of his head.

"How you doin', Little Man?" Kirby inquired as he bent over to kiss Yvette on her forehead.

"Hey Kirby," Yvette shot back with excitement.

"Where you guys comin' from?"

"Aunt Traci's house," Dannon answered as Kirby let him down.

"Is it hot enough for you guys?" Kirby asked as the perspiration drowned his body.

"It's too hot. I'm gettin' ready to go back inside." Yvette replied and wiped her forehead with the back of her hand.

"How's your mother? Give her my regards."

"Okay, we will. See you later."

Kirby made his way back to his buddies on the bleachers when he peered past the park and noticed a very shapely female wearing a pink tank top and matching shorts.

Big Joe noticed Kirby's trance and followed his fixation.

"V-v-very n-n-nice, I-I-I would l-l-love to walk her home."

"That's Angela!" Dexter said.

"Angela?" Kirby said and sprinted off toward her. Dexter and Big Joe tried unsuccessfully to restrain him.

Kirby reached Angela within a twinkling of an eye,

and she immediately protested his existence.

"Angela. Wait."

"Why did you mention my name to the police, Kirby? I'm a potential suspect now. I can't believe you."

"Look Angela," Kirby tried to reason.

"Kirby, you weasel. I loved Bennett. Why would I want to kill him? That doesn't make any sense to me."

Kirby's gentle yank of Angela's arm was enough to get her to stop and give ear.

"I'm sorry Angela, but when the cops asked me for names of people who I thought could've or had problems with Bennett, I remembered you—the day in the hall when you threatened him over the deal that happened with you and Mr. Whitby."

"Kirby, that was nothing. I was only angry for a second, no matter what the deal was. I was only angry for a short time."

"I had to do what I thought was best. I told the truth. I mean, like where were you anyway when everything happened?"

"What!" Angela answered in surprise and shock. "Check the photo in the newspaper the day it happened. I was standing right in front of the podium listening to Bennett's speech just like everyone else. What are you crazy or something?"

"Well, I was asked questions so I answered them. That was my man."

"Kirby, I was done. I was embarrassed," Angela said after listening to Kirby's reasoning. "I was also very scared getting yelled at like that by the police."

"Angela."

"They had a bright light shining in my face and a tape recorder. It was a mess. I had to get a lawyer, and my mother was a basket case."

"Hey, I'm sorry but..."

"Oh yeah, and as far as Mr. Whitby is concerned, he was questioned too."

"He was?"

"Of course he was but he had an alibi. He was out of town attending his nephew's wedding in Philly."

"But..."

"Listen, Kirby," Angela said, in a tone that expressed a lack of tolerance for Kirby's public informal interrogation. "Let the police handle it. Let them handle it, please. Good-bye!"

Kirby gazed back at the park but his boys were nowhere to be found. Instead of retreating home to escape the bristling sun, he chose his course of action to be the Mount Vernon police station.

Nine

The hike to the police station was a long tedious process, which left Kirby soaked, dehydrated, and exhausted. The red brick station house was located downtown adjacent to city hall, the place where Bennett was fatally wounded. Kirby made his way over to a white-haired police officer that was making time with a cup of coffee and a glazed donut.

Inside, the station had the look of an old-time jail house with paint chipped walls, rotary dial telephones, rusted metal desks, and graffiti smeared cells that housed ten to twelve prisoners at one time.

"Officer Pickman?" Kirby asked after reading the stubby fellow's badge.

"Yes, young man, what can I do for you?"

"Well you can start off by tellin' me if you've made any arrests yet."

"Arrests?"

"Yeah," Kirby said with volume that drew attention. "Do you have any arrests in the Bennett Wilson murder?"

The answer Kirby received was not the one he wanted, but he figured as much. In a fit of rage, he stormed out of the station mumbling unpleasantries under his breath.

"Kirby!" Detective Bill Baines barked before Kirby reached the corner. Baines was formerly one of Mount Vernon's two truant officers. He stood six-feet tall, with a baldhead, and he flexed 23-inch biceps.

"I don't have anything to say."

Baines stopped in his tracks and looked at Kirby as he continued to walk away, "Kirby, talk to me...Now!"

"Mr. Baines..."

"Hey listen, we're doing all we can under the circumstances."

"Circumstances! Please, save it."

"Now hold it right there. I've known you both a long time. I know your families. You know that if I had any information, anything at all, you'd know about it. But, right now, they're no suspects."

"No suspects?"

"None. Every name you gave us, and every person we've checked out, came out clean; had an airtight alibi. Either they were there at the scene with witnesses, or they were out of town.

Either way Kirby, they are no longer considered suspects. I know he wasn't into any organized crime or anything but, his death, especially the way it was done, is very strange. Strange. But we're still working on it, you can rest assured."

Kirby felt the police let him down, Mr. Baines included. He had no more interest in continuing the discussion. He reluctantly shook Mr. Baines' hand and went about his way.

# # #

After drowning his sorrows with a bottle of bourbon, Kirby found himself roaming the streets.

It was close to midnight as he drifted around chasing pink elephants until he reached the Yonkers city limits, the South Yonkers city limits to be exact. He remembered that Shorty lived there and usually hung out at Slappy's pool hall, so he staggered along.

He reached Slappy's pool hall and was greeted by a cloud of cheap cigar smoke, the sound of the Temptations blasting from the jukebox, and the knocking of pool balls against each other.

Kirby saw Slappy standing behind the counter giving change and selling soft drinks. Slappy was a middle-aged man around fifty years of age, short, semi-bald and wore a white T-shirt and brown vest daily. Slappy, in his younger days, was a bartender and stand-up comedian. The 'Slappy' label came as a colloquialism for 'knee slapper.'

"Slappy, let me have one of those Coca-Colas please."

"Kirby, my man, I haven't seen you in a while. What brings you this way?"

Kirby started sipping his soda, and before answering, he had to cover his mouth to catch some that tried to escape.

He Was My Hero, Too

"I have some business to tend to."

"Business? What kind of business?" Slappy inquired as they both turned to the sudden cluster of noise.

Shorty Stokes and his mob had burst onto the scene. As they entered, the whole place went quiet. One could hear a pin drop.

"That's my business," Kirby answered, putting down his soda and making his way towards them.

"Kirby!"

Given to drink as he was, Kirby still remembered the quintet, especially the tallest one with the chrome dome that wore a scar on his forehead. He and Bennett beat them senseless. The one who had the bushy afro looked as though he never recovered from the broken nose he suffered at the hands of Bennett.

He caught a glimpse of Shorty, his intended target, and noticed his two front teeth had not been replaced. Bennett really cracked him good. The other two tried to front their coolness by sporting dark shades in the dead of night.

"Shorty! What's up! I want to talk to you!"

Shorty, who started licking his chops and rubbing his hands together, responded, "I've been waitin' for this moment a long time." Kirby's stomach was not ready to receive the impact of Shorty's punch. Kirby grimaced in pain, as he doubled over. The twenty or so patrons scattered the pool hall like roaches fleeing a suddenly lit room.

Two of the men, the one with the shades and the

one with the bald head, snatched Kirby from behind. Shorty took the opportunity to whack Kirby with all his might. Blood began purging from Kirby's nose and mouth as he felt himself not far from unconsciousness. He felt a cutting pain in the back of his head. The slap from Shorty's pool stick sent shock waves from the crown of Kirby's head to the balls of his feet.

"That's enough!" Slappy yelled. "Stop it before I call the police!"

"Shut your mouth, before you get some of this too," Shorty snapped back.

One of the hoods seized a slumped-over Kirby and threw him head first into a wood-paneled wall. Shorty and his four horsemen laughed ecstatically and made their way over to him.

Armed with a .22-caliber pistol, Shorty asked coldheartedly, "You ready to go home now, punk?"

"No," Kirby faintly answered.

Shorty continued laughing as he removed bullets from his gun. "You wanna meet your maker?"

"I don't want to die," Kirby said through a stream of heavy tears. "Please don't kill me."

"Aw, he's begging for his life," Shorty said. "You know how to play Russian roulette?"

Kirby could not respond. The fear, which shuddered through his body, had paralyzed his senses.

Shorty knelt down next to a fallen Kirby. He spent the chamber of the .22-caliber handgun and forced it up against Kirby's temple. "If I pull this trigger and you're not shot, you won't die. But, if you are shot...bye-bye."

The first click, which came from an empty chamber, caused Kirby's senses to return as he attempted to jump out of his skin. Shorty then rose to his feet cackling again with his friends as they watched Kirby beg for his life.

"Please don't kill me," Kirby said squinting his eyes trying to regain a focus. "Don't shoot me, I don't want to die."

"Shut up! Just shut up! You should've thought about that before you came lookin' for me all incorrect."

Shorty bowed down and unmercifully yanked the trigger. Once more like a jackrabbit, Kirby jumped on cue. The end of this jump, however was followed by a relieved bladder and uninvited moisture in his pants.

"Enough!" Simon shouted as he, Big Willie, and Little Tiny Smalls entered the pool hall. "I said, that's enough, didn't you hear me?"

Shorty stood up and snickered, "Get 'um!" He then motioned with his head; first to his henchmen then to their intended target.

"I need this exercise," Willie said as he uncorked a punch that pummeled the hood with the scar on his face. The guy was hit so hard his whole body stiffened before he fell. One of the shaded characters let out a loud roar and picked up a pool stick and charged after Little Tiny. Little Tiny, undaunted, jumped into a fencing position with his walking cane. That is until he grew tired of the shenanigans and dropped the guy with a blow to the head.

Willie ran over to the other shaded punk who was, at this time, frightened out of his wits. Willie elected not to use his hands. He simply head-butted him instead.

The last one, the one sporting the afro—maybe he had too much hair on his head—foolishly hopped on Little Tiny's back and began beating him upside the head. Little Tiny remained calm. There was no need to worry. He simply let go of his cane, grabbed the man by the hands and flipped him over.

For some strange reason only known to him, the guy would not quit. He exploded off his back and lunged toward him. Forthwith, Little Tiny picked up his cane, broke into a batting stance—reminiscent of Hank Aaron waiting for a fast ball down the middle of the plate—and whacked him on the noggin.

Shorty saw the destruction of his men and felt helpless. He pulled his piece on Simon and said, "I'll take you outta here, right now!"

"Young boy, you ain't got the guts. And," Simon said as he, Big Willie and Little Tiny Smalls showed off their pieces of armor, "you certainly don't have the hardware." Shorty felt defeated and sucked his snaggy teeth.

"Get that toy from him, Willie," Simon said as he walked over to Kirby.

Willie snatched the gun away from Shorty, looked at it, frowned, and pimp-slapped him. The smack was really hard and really loud. Shorty would have done the United States gymnastics team very proud in the Olympics. He did a pirouette, a somersault, and a dismount over not one but two pool tables. Thus, another tooth was lost. Willie laughed and yelled, "Nine point five!" Then he gave Simon a five and handed him the gun.

"Thanks Willie," Simon said accepting it. "Do me a favor, you and Tiny take this trash out of here. I'll see how little man is doing."

Slappy suddenly reappeared from behind the counter and asked, "Is it over yet?"

Simon looked at him and became furious and clamored, "You were back there all this time and let this happen?"

"I, I, I, I..."

"You could've at least called the police!"

"I, I, I, I..."

"Forget him, Simon," Willie said waving his hand at Slappy. "You know he ain't nothing but a washerwoman anyway."

Simon reversed his attention to a half-dazed Kirby. He reached into his jacket pocket and pulled out a white handkerchief. Kirby resisted but then acceded to Simon's persistence. Kirby was totally perplexed, more from Simon's assistance then the battering he took.

"Fear not, man. I'm not gonna hurt you."

Kirby shoved the bloodied handkerchief in front of Simon's face.

"No, you can keep it," Simon said with a smile. "I know you're probably wondering what I'm doing here."

"The thought did cross my mind."

"The answer is, I like you, kid. I think you have a lot of guts. But, as you just saw, guts could've gotten you killed."

"I was just tryin' to find out who killed Bennett. No one is givin' me answers. Why am I tellin' you this anyway?" Kirby said as he grimaced and grabbed his right side.

"Your ribs are probably broken."

"No kiddin', Sherlock."

Simon was slightly insulted by Kirby's remark, but managed a smile and offered, "That's okay. I can take it. But you have to let the police handle this. Didn't the cop tell you so earlier today?"

Kirby looked at Simon and his eyes told him what he was thinking.

"Yeah, I was following you. I've been keeping an eye out. I wanted you protected. I figured you might run into something like this sooner or later. It was just a matter of time."

Gratitude got the best of Kirby as he brought about a smile through his swollen, crimson lips. "What took you so long, then?"

"You want to know the truth. Well...Willie had to get something to eat. Don't laugh, you're gonna hurt yourself. Listen. I know you may not want to hear this but you need to let the police handle this investigation. This thing is bigger than you.

"The way Bennett was killed, in my opinion, has all

the makings of a hit. I know he wasn't into anything heavy but it smells like one. The cops won't tell you."

"How and why do you figure?"

"It was done from long range. It was as if it were done from another part of the city. The gun or rifle used was a high powered one," Simon said as he looked at the gun he still had in his possession. "Something high powered, nothing like this toy thing here. Besides...Shorty and his guys are chumps. Look, see, no bullets. He tried that Russian roulette garbage with you just to scare you. He wasn't gonna shoot you."

"Well," Kirby said as he eyed down his soggy pants leg, "he certainly had me fooled."

"Let's get outta here. Let me take you home. Or do you want me to take you to the hospital?"

"No hospital, but," Kirby said attempting to get to his feet, with little success, "I can make it."

"Yeah, right. I'm taking you home."

Simon helped Kirby to his feet. Kirby left the pool hall hanging onto Simon's shoulder.

Ten

JULY 1973

"Son, my God, what happened to you?" A frightened Lois asked as she caught Kirby in her arms.

"Momma, I had a little trouble that's all."

"Trouble? What kind of trouble? You look like you're hurt. I'm calling the police."

"No Momma, no. It's been takin' care of already."

Mrs. Maxwell sat her devastated and wounded son down on the couch before going to the kitchen. Mrs. Maxwell pulled out a box of Arm-in-Hammer baking soda and a yellow plastic pale from the closet and filled it with warm water.

Kirby begged his mother not to call the police or the ambulance as she was patting his bruises trying to soothe and ease the pain.

At the end she dropped her quest but not until after Kirby explained what was going on. Her mystery son was not to be any more. She wanted and demanded answers. But she started out by urging him in a very

He Was My Hero, Too

stern matter, "Kirby, you have to stop this drinking. Please stop it. Son, if you have problems, I don't care what they are; come and talk to me about them. I know you are a man, and you have your own personal things going, but son, I'm your mother and I love you with all my heart. I'll listen to you even if I don't understand you. I'm here for you."

"I know Momma, I..."

"And if I weren't here, if God decided to take my life, I know someone else will emerge in your life for you to talk to. Please, please stop drinking. And for God's sake, please don't start doing no drugs."

Kirby, at last, came clean with his mother and told her all of what he was going through since his good friend's death. He gave her details of events up until the hour when Shorty and his boys beat him to a pulp. Kirby also confessed he was rescued by a person who he wished would die a vicious death.

"Kirby, you have to stop snooping around for answers about Bennett."

"Yes Momma, I..."

"Son," Mrs. Maxwell grabbed Kirby by his shoulders. "I don't want to lose you.

Mrs. Maxwell turned her head towards the living room window. "Every night I could just hear Betty crying." Mrs. Maxwell continued, talking more to herself than to Kirby, as she stared into the abyss of the night.

Kirby gave his mother a blank and confused look.

"No, Son, not literally. I mean I could hear her soul

crying out to her son. Bennett was her child, her first-born. Kirby, I don't want to lose you that way. So please keep yourself out of trouble and let the police handle it. We all hurt but what can we realistically do?"

"Momma, I miss him. I miss Bennett. Every time the telephone rings or there is a knock on the door. I'm just hopin' and wishin' it could be him sayin', 'Kirb it was all a joke, let's go play ball or get something to eat.' But, then I go to his gravesite and see his name engraved on that tombstone."

Kirby laid his head in his mother's lap. "Momma, why did somebody have to kill him? He never hurt nobody. And why can't they find out who did it? Why? Momma? Why?"

Kirby and his mother rapped until the early hours of the morning. He shared his immediate and future intentions. Kirby mentioned he was considering joining the Navy. She vehemently opposed it. But, he stated that he wanted to make a man out of himself and that was the best way.

"Momma, I believe in myself and I think I'll be all right."

"Son, I believe in you too, but war is just what it is...war."

"We're not fighting right now, Momma," Kirby said as confidently as possible. "Listen, I don't want to die, but I remember a conversation I had with Bennett. I told him when I do die, I'd like to die with some dignity and not like some animal in the streets, or strung out on drugs."

He Was My Hero, Too

"Son, I'm so scared of losing you, but on the other hand, I am so proud of you. You are a man now. You've grown up right before my very eyes," Mrs. Maxwell ended the sentence with a kiss to Kirby's forehead.

"Momma, now," Kirby said playfully, "don't get all mushy and stuff."

"I'm so proud of you."

"Momma..."

"Have you told Kathy, yet?"

"No," Kirby sighed. "I haven't, you're the first person I've mentioned this too."

Mrs. Maxwell stared into Kirby's eyes at the mere mention of Kathy's name was broached. "You really love Kathy don't you?"

"Yeah Momma, I do."

"How do you think her parents will feel about it?"

"Well, her father was in the Navy," Kirby said with a sly smile. "That's my ace-in-the-hole."

"You are so crazy," Mrs. Maxwell pushed off on Kirby playfully. "Just be yourself." Mrs. Maxwell then reverted to the previous subject. "I trust you've checked long and hard on the Navy thing? When would you ship out? What's going on?"

"Momma," Kirby said grim-faced. "I think I'd be shippin' out in a month or so after boot camp. I think I need to get outta here as soon as possible."

"So how are you proposing to get married any time soon or are you?"

"I'm figuring six to seven months."

"Kirby," Mrs. Maxwell dead-panned. "Please tell me Kathy isn't pregnant."

"Yeah Momma."

"Yeah?"

"No, I mean no. She's not pregnant."

"Whew," Mrs. Maxwell breathed a sigh of relief. "Thank you, Son, thank you. Get yourselves together first, then have children. Anyway, let me go and finish cooking."

# # #

Two weeks had flown by and Kirby was still bedridden and mending his wounds. Kathy's parents had already given the okay on his marriage proposal, so his mood was better. He was viewing his favorite show on television when his mother told him he had visitors.

"Hey, Buddy," Dexter said as he and Big Joe entered. He sat on the edge of Kirby's bed while Big Joe grabbed a fold-up chair from the hallway. "How're you feelin' today?"

"I'm all right. I think I'm startin' to feel normal again. Thanks for askin', but how're you guys doin'?"

"B-b-better th-th-than y-y-you is, of-of-of co-co-course."

"Of-of-of co-co-course," Kirby chimed in.

"Now, you guys don't start, we came here to cheer you up and to see how you were gettin' along before we all take off out of here. I'm leavin' soon, you're leavin' soon, and Joe's leavin'. Who knows when we'll see

He Was My Hero, Too

each other again—and for how long."

"Dex," Kirby said and started laughing softly, "you gettin' misty on us?"

Dexter took a pillow and smashed Kirby, sending him flat on his bed. "I ain't gettin' misty. I'm just gonna miss you guys, that's all."

"Aw, th-th-that's..."

"Don't start Joe, don't you start," Dexter said.

The like-minded friends had been watching the remaining bits of the 'Julia Show' and were chatting easily, until Dexter remembered something. "Guess what," he said with visible excitement. "Guess what. Good news!"

"What? What already?" Kirby said.

"Simon got arrested the other day."

"What!"

"Yeah, the man is doin' time right now in Sing-Sing."

"What did he do?"

"He punched out a cop."

"Get outta here. Which cop? What happened?"

"You know the cop. He's stationed on Gramatan Avenue," Dexter said snapping his finger trying to remember the man-in-blue's name. "What's his name?"

"Of-Of-Officer Ja-Ja-Jack Rhoden."

"Yeah Joe, him. Well..."

"He's a racist," Kirby said. "He did the city a favor. He..."

"Let me tell you what happened," Dexter said and stood up to demonstrate the act he witnessed.

"Policeman Rhoden saw Simon's car. Simon had double-parked and apparently gone inside Joe's Pizzeria. But he put his hazard lights on."

"He was drivin'? Where was Willie?"

"I don't know but Simon was alone. Anyway, Rhoden saw him go inside but he waited until Simon came out to start writin' him a ticket. Simon didn't protest. He took it in stride and put his hand out for the ticket, but Rhoden snatched it back. He snatched it back and started walkin' around the car. I guess he was checkin' for violations or somethin'. But, he didn't find anything so he came back to Simon and shoved the ticket in his chest. Then, here's the kicker," Dexter started laughing. "He called him the dreaded 'N' word."

"What? He called him a Negro?"

"No man, not that 'N' word, da udder one. And for good measure, he added he was a lowdown and dirty one. He called him a 'dirty ni...'"

"I know he don't like our kind...but, get outta here. For real?"

"I kid you not. Man. Simon dropped him somethin' serious, though. I mean he had Rhoden on queer street."

"What are you talkin' about?" Kirby asked.

Dexter and Big Joe started chortling uncontrollably as Dexter tried to get the words out. Kirby himself started cackling too.

"Well," Dexter managed to say. "Just before Rhoden went out cold, after he hit the ground, rolled over and started yellin' and screamin', 'Where's my badge!

He Was My Hero, Too

Where's my badge!' Then he cried out for his Momma."

"What?"

"I hadn't laughed so hard in years."

"What did Simon do?"

"Check this out, he lights up a cigar."

"Get out."

"Just like Red Auerbach does when he wins a championship, and merely sits on top of his hood waitin' for the cops to come. He didn't even try to run or get away. And I heard Rhoden's jaw is broken in three places."

"Man," Kirby said nonchalantly. "I guess I would've ended up in jail too."

"Kirby, I thought you'd be jumpin' for joy about it. Simon's finally in the clink. The joint! The hoosegal! Up the river! The big house! And he's gonna do some serious time, man. He's lookin' at, at least five to ten. You're not happy? I thought you'd be jumpin' for joy."

Kirby who had been staring down at his pillow lifted his head and said, "You say he's in Sing-Sing right?"

"What's wrong with you? You find religion on us Kirby? You gone soft in your old age?"

"No Dex. I guess I didn't tell you everything that exactly happened at Slappy's," Kirby said and then explained the whole deal to Joe and Dex. They came away equally impressed with Simon and felt sorry the way they had been gloating over it.

Kirby woke up the next morning feeling much better, so he decided he would do some much needed ripping and running. He stopped by a pawn shop and selected a set of wedding rings for himself and Kathy. He stopped by the Naval recruiter's office to finalize the paper work. He also dropped by his mother's place of employment—Sears's department store—and delivered her a dozen roses, for her 50th birthday.

But Kirby's day was not done, for he would board a bus, to Ossining, New York. The place where Sing-Sing prison is located. Sing-Sing is the place where Simon would have to call home for some time.

Kirby knew he needed permission to see Simon since a regular off-the-street visitation would be prohibited. Since Simon had no idea to put him on the list, Kirby used another method. He knew one of the correction officers from their days at the Boy's Club. Kirby figured the club connection would suffice and afford the favor needed to get him in to see Simon.

It worked. Kirby had to pose as Simon's son from California who came to New York looking for his father. After being fingerprinted and going through the usual process—the strip search—Kirby took his place behind the telephone and two-way glass blockade awaiting Simon's arrival.

The visiting room was painted in a cold, light green color. The paint was not only cold looking; it was chipped giving it more of an unwelcome appeal. There were ten visiting stations equipped with cushioned chairs, ashtrays, and telephones for direct communication. The high glass blockade made any physical contact impossible.

He Was My Hero, Too

A guard patrolled the premises to keep order and to make sure none of the prisoners got out of hand with their emotions.

A half hour passed and a surprised Simon arrived clad in orange prison fatigues.

Simon picked up the telephone and motioned to Kirby to do likewise.

"I'm glad to see you, but what are you doing here? And how did you get in?"

"I pulled a few strings. I know a few people around here. But, I came to see how you were doin'. How you comin' along."

Simon sat back in his seat and unleashed a colossal smile and said, "I've had better days. I'm not exactly used to this. Being confined and all, but I'm coming along. I'm coming along just fine. Thanks for asking."

Kirby had put his head down seemingly fighting for words to say. Simon noticed the anguish on Kirby's face and decided he would help him along.

"Is there something you want to say to me? I mean you have this look on your face as if you're constipated."

Kirby raised his head and managed a smile and added, "Yeah Simon, I never thought I'd be tellin' you this but, I'm grateful and I want to thank you for comin' to my aid. You saved my life and I appreciate it."

"I told you before he took the bullets out, didn't I?"

"Yeah, but as scared as I was, I could've died from a heart attack."

"Okay, now that your life has been saved, what are

you gonna do with it?"

"What do you mean?"

"I mean are you gonna make something out of yourself, or are you gonna end up like me. Those streets don't have anything for you. Trust me."

Kirby had a bemused look on his face.

"It's me talking," Simon said. "From my mouth to your ears. What are you gonna do with yourself?"

"I can't believe you're talkin' like this. I mean, you?"

"Young fella, there's a lot about me you just don't know. You probably wouldn't believe it anyway."

A curious Kirby asked, "Try me."

"Some other time, some other time. Listen," Simon said and pointed at Kirby. "Take my advice, stop what you're doing. I'm talking about the drinking and whatnot." Simon paused a moment as if a beam of light had shone upon him, then continued, "You didn't take the smack you bought the other day, did you?"

Kirby gave Simon another bemused look.

"Yeah, young fella, I knew about it. And you don't have to worry about him selling any more in Mount Vernon. Stop the nonsense and go to college or something. Get out of town for a while. Give yourself a chance, man. Do the right thing."

"Well, I enlisted into the Navy."

"There are other options you know."

"I know but I'll take my chances. I'm man enough to handle whatever comes."

Kirby and Simon confabulated a little while longer

He Was My Hero, Too

switching subjects back and forth. Kirby had urged Simon to seek help from witnesses. After all, he knew Dexter was there and saw what had happened. Simon refused. He felt there was no chance of winning despite who saw what. He pressed on the fact to not being considered a community role model. He also cited, especially in Dexter's case, he was getting ready for college, and coming back and forth to court for someone he hated for a time would not be the wise thing to do. He stated he too was man enough to take whatever came his way. He was ready to take his medicine and his punishment. He knew his lawyer would do all he could, but he expected the worse. He conceded breaking a cop's jaw was not something you can just get away with.

Kirby lost track of the time sitting and chatting with his newfound friend. Moments later a guard declared visiting hours were over.

"You gonna be all right, man?" Kirby asked with genuine concern.

"I'll be fine, young fella. You make sure you take care of yourself."

The guard impatiently tapped Kirby on his shoulder.

"I guess I better get outta here. Take care or yourself, Simon. I'll keep in touch."

"Okay, that'll be cool. And I'll do the same. Hey, congratulations on your upcoming nuptials. I hope you all the best. Really."

Kirby got up and made his way towards the door. A tapping sound caused Kirby to stop. It was Simon frantically pounding on the glass. Kirby looked at the guard who was dressed in his blue uniform readied with a gun and a nightstick and handcuffs to get his approval. The guard, reading Kirby's thoughts frowned momentarily as he was the last one to leave, reluctantly but affirmatively nodded his head. Kirby went back to the station and picked up the telephone.

"What's up, Simon?"

Simon, feeling emotional pressed his fist against the glass. Kirby followed suit and placed his also, solidifying the bond between them.

"Thanks for coming to see about me. I really appreciate it. You really didn't have to do it."

"No problem."

"Promise me something," Simon said and looked Kirby straight in the eye. "I know I said this before to you, but I mean it. I want you to make something of yourself. Do you hear me? Make something of yourself."

"I will Simon, I will. I promise."

Eleven

NOVEMBER 1984

"Simon, you ready yet?" Kirby asked entering his office with Kirby Jr. and Bennie tagging along. "The game starts in 45 minutes. I don't want to miss the tip-off."

Simon was on the telephone, and from the looks of things, the conversation seemed to be very serious. Kirby caught the hint of Simon's look and pushed his sons out the door.

"You guys go shoot some baskets until we're ready."

"Aw, Dad, come on," said Junior who was the spitting image of his father—head shape, body structure and nose—but had his mother's light brown eyes. "Do we have to?"

"Yeah, you have to. Now go on."

As the boy exited, Kirby focused his attention back to Simon who was still engrossed in heavy dialog.

Several more minutes elapsed before Simon disconnected his party over Ma Bell. He motioned to Kirby to shut the door.

"That was Harry Hooch. The guy I was telling you about who could dig up some stuff about Bennett's murder."

"Yeah," an eager Kirby answered. "What's up? What does he have for us?"

"Kirby, as I suspected all along, Bennett was the victim of a hit, a hired high-priced hit. Nothing the average person would be able to afford. I mean this was a high-priced hit. It had to be out-of-towners; I didn't hear anything. I mean I didn't hear anything on the streets about any local muscle doing it."

"What!" A chill ran up through Kirby as he sat down.

"Just as I suspected way back when," Simon chimed in. "I'm sorry."

Kirby ran his hands through his hair and massaged his face before responding, "Who? Why? Who on earth would put out a hit like that on a high school kid? I mean Bennett. He wasn't in to anything that would necessitate him being taken out."

"Listen, Harry may be on to something. He doesn't have any names yet, but he feels he's getting close. That's why I was talking with him so long."

"What does he have in mind?"

"You're not gonna like this, but he said we should seek the help of the mayor."

Kirby again made a gesture with his head that clearly showed his dismay over the idea. But before he could get the word "no" out of his mouth, Simon reminded him, the idea was to find Bennett's killer, not to make friends with anyone. After careful thought, Kirby knew giving in was the best thing. The two men agreed but decided to table the discussion for later.

Suddenly Kirby's kids crashed in the office, "Dad, let's go!" Junior said. "Daddy, we're gonna miss the start of the most important game of the year!"

"We only have 20 minutes."

"I know, Son," Kirby said with a sly grin. "Mount Vernon verses New Ro, survival of the fittest? Best men win? It's not just war...it's Armageddon."

"Daddy," Bennie said, not appreciating being teased.

"Hey guys, I was on the team before, remember?"

"That was so long ago, Daddy, things are different now."

Simon and Kirby looked at one another and exchanged grins. Simon gave Kirby the signal to keep quiet, as he did not feel like a huge debate.

Cognizant of the time and importance of not losing the love of his family because of a game, Kirby, Simon and the boys made their way to Kirby's car, and off they went to the Mount Vernon High School gymnasium.

The high school parking lot was full of loud cheers for the game that had not yet begun. The intensity level was as thick as the darkness of the night. The moment Kirby purchased the tickets a surge went through his body. He was unsure if it was from the unnerving news he found out about Bennett or the excitement about the game itself. He tried to put the news about Bennett behind him, for the time being. But it was utterly impossible. Since he was returning, after a twelve-year absence, to the gym where Bennett made his name.

Apart from a new paint job, Kirby saw that the place still looked the same. The 1973 championship banner with which Bennett single handily won hung high above on the wall to the left of the gym as you entered. He noticed the school had retired Bennett's number '42' jersey.

The crowd was making way to their seats in the bleachers as the cheerleaders from both schools shouted 'rah-rah' chants to one another. Town political figures from both cities, including the mayors, were in attendance. Among the assemblage of students and townspeople, scouts from both the college ranks as well as the National Basketball Association could be spotted jotting down notes.

The game was set to start in a matter of minutes so both teams were vigorously warming up in their lay-up drills. But out of all the players, Dannon was absolutely marvelous. He was wreaking havoc putting on a dunking exhibition that would have made Dr. J envious. He was coming down on the hoop so strong the basket would shake uncontrollably for several seconds after he left his mark. The loud thud he made upon his descent would startle inattentive fans.

At last, the showdown was about to begin. This game was not for all the marbles. But, it was for a whole bunch of them and bragging rights. Both teams were

He Was My Hero, Too

destined to make the playoffs. They each carried undefeated records going into the game, with Mount Vernon winning ten and New Rochelle eleven.

The ten combatants met at the circle of honor and exchanged the traditional handshakes. It was obvious though, that these guys really did not care for each other. Dannon made his way over to New Rochelle's star forward and defensive whiz, Chandler McMurtry. He stood a rugged six foot seven, 210 pounds. He was probably a tad shorter than that, but because he sported one of those 'hi-lo' fade haircuts, it was hard to actually tell. The rest of McMurtry's crew consisted of six-foot-three point guard supreme, Gregory Starks; all-county shooting guard who stood six-foot-four, Nick "Mercedes" Benns; Josh Baxter, at six-foot-nine was the big center in the middle; and six-foot-six sharp shooting forward, "Triple O-seven", O'Brien O'Hara O'Sullivan. No fooling, that was his name. His parents, Oliver and Olga had this fascination with names that started with the letter O.

The Mount Vernon quintet was no slouch either. Dannon had plenty of firepower to go along with him. His best friend on the team, Jordan "Fleet Feet" Alexander, was the point guard. At six-feet-four, he was considered the quickest and the strongest point guard in the state. Manual Rivera, who at six-foot-one; played out of position at the shooting guard spot. Handling the basketball was not his forte, but because of his sweet shooting stroke, Coach Dee had to put him in the starting line-up. At center, Ranfi Hutu at six-foot-ten, manned, controlled, and policed the paint area. He averaged an unprecedented twelve blocks per game to go along with eighteen rebounds. Rounding out the top five was fellow all-state honoree, six-foot-five forward Ray Richardson.

"McMurtry," Dannon said as he was tying a knot into his uniform short pants. "I hear you been talkin' trash in the paper about how you were gonna hold me down to ten points. Is that right?"

"Yeah," McMurtry said as he rose to his feet to look Dannon straight in the eye. "I believe I said somethin' to that effect. I don't see where I could've been misquoted."

"Well, did you mean ten points for the game or for the first quarter? I think your mouth may be tryin' to write checks that your butt may not be able to cash."

"What a wonderful sayin', did your Momma teach you that?"

Dannon lost his cool and had to be restrained by his teammate, Jordan.

"Don't get yourself kicked out of the game on my account. Stay awhile and take the whuppin' like men. Or ladies, whatever you prefer."

"What's all the conversation about?" The ref with the prison striped shirt said. "Let's play ball!"

Dannon started fuming and could not wait until the ref threw the ball up into the air. The ref did his part and Mount Vernon took control. Jordan handed the ball off to Dannon who immediately called for a clear-out play. McMurtry jumped into his standardized trademark defensive stance and began yelling some unpleasant things at him. Dannon somehow kept his poise notwithstanding the force of adrenaline eating away at him. With head movement, he faked left and went right with a speed dribble. After shifting his body weight, McMurtry smiled, caught up to Dannon, and again yelled harsh things at him. Dannon bounced the ball between his legs in a stutter step crossover dribble fashion and juke faked again. McMurtry went flying past Dannon, but not before Dannon was able to tell him, "have a nice flight, Baby," before swishing home a jump shot.

On defense he called Ray Richardson off. He wanted to guard him.

Coach Dee could care less. He knew of Dannon's competitive fire so long as he stayed within the team concept. Dannon was careful not to get in a "heavy" trash talking episode; not with the horde of scouts in the stands watching his every move.

"I got him, Ray, take mine!" Dannon was licking his chops.

McMurtry stationed on the left baseline posted Dannon up. Someone yelled out, "I got your help," to Dannon as McMurtry tried to create space for himself. Dannon refused it as he had his own plan for defending McMurty. He waited until McMurtry felt good and comfortable enough to attempt his shot. Dannon faked as if he was getting beaten and backed away lamely. Instantly, McMurtry squared up to take his shot. But, Dannon suddenly appeared out of nowhere and pinned the rising shot up against the backboard. The force of the block was so great, during a time-out, Jordan told Dannon he thought he heard air seep out of the ball.

Mount Vernon was back on offense. Jordan yelled out the "three down power" play, which called for Dannon to post up his man on the right box—baseline, once everyone cleared out. Dannon took in a deep breath and readied himself to receive the pass. The moment he got the ball, you could hear the fierce rumble of the crowd. Fans in anticipation of something great started stomping their feet in a stampede-type fashion. The sound of the earthquake had the building rocking.

Dannon asked his defender, Chandler McMurtry, "You got me, boy?"

"I'm in your back pocket, son. Bring it on."

Dannon obliged. He head faked left and dropped stepped right. McMurtry in one fell-swoop hit the floor as if someone had clocked him. Dannon peered briefly at his fallen foe as he began his ascent into the air. Upon reaching his peak, Dannon cocked the ball behind his head and slammed it through the hoop. The New Rochelle coach felt he was losing his team and was propelled to call a time out.

The onslaught continued with Mount Vernon winning the game 101-78. Dannon ended the game with 47

He Was My Hero, Too

points, fifteen rebounds and ten assists. And what should not be lost in all of this is Dannon, after he stripped McMurtry of the ball at least a dozen times, held him down to eight points for the game.

On the contest's final buzzer, while the Mount Vernon fans were going wild, McMurtry made his way over to Dannon and allowed good sportsmanship to take over. After all, they were one-time teammates on the Westchester County AAU basketball team. Dannon wished him luck throughout the rest of their season, except if they met again of course.

Kirby who sat in the stands felt all the virtue of the team's win as if he were part of it himself; he hugged and high-fived his two sons to death.

Suddenly, a sharp pain pierced through his head, which was so severe he felt himself starting to grow faint.

Dannon was making his way to the locker room when Jay Rock who was with two of his comrades, yelled something to him. Dannon changed courses and proceeded to go over to him.

Simon saw it and told Kirby he would be back.

"Jay Rock," Simon said giving him a menacing look. "Now I told you before..."

"Simon, slow down. I was just tellin' him nice game, that's all."

"What's goin' on, Simon?" A befuddled Dannon asked.

"Nothing. How you getting home?"

"Momma and I are gettin' a ride with Aunt Traci."

"Okay, go on and get yourself changed and I'll see you tomorrow," Simon said exchanging dirty looks with Jay Rock and his partners as he shoved Dannon away.

One of Jay Rock's companions whispered something into his ear and the two started snickering. As Simon walked away, he caught Junior flailing his arms frantically. Simon shot up the bleachers like a cannon.

"Kirby, you all right?"

"The pain in my head. It's killing me, Simon."

"I'm taking you to the hospital. I'm not waiting for an ambulance."

"Wait a second, I don't want anybody to see me like this."

"We're parked in the back. Let's go out the back door. Come on man, I got you."

The ride to the Mount Vernon hospital was a blur as Simon took every light and ran every stop sign that was in his path.

When Kirby came to, he found himself on his back stretched out on a gurney with a doctor's flashlight shining brightly in his eyes.

"Can you hear, son?" The doctor asked. "You're in the emergency room."

Kirby's eyes were unfocused as his mind began to wander. He began to have the same sickening feeling he experienced when Bennett laid bleeding profusely from a bullet wound.

"I can hear you."

He Was My Hero, Too

Just as Kirby answered, he heard someone to his left sniffling. He turned to see who it was and saw that it was his wife.

"Kathy, what are you doing here? And where're the kids?"

Kathy took time to wipe her face and gather herself before she answered, "Simon took them home and put them to bed. We didn't think they should be here."

"You guys didn't call my mother, did you?"

"Of course we did. We had to. And she's on her way over. She should be here any minute."

Kirby began to get anxious at the prospect of his mother seeing him, he was.

"Don't get yourself excited, son. Relax," the doctor said as he removed his thick bifocal glasses. Kirby thought to himself, either the man got dressed in the dark or those glasses must not be doing any good. The doctor was dressed in black, white, and green-stripped psychedelic pants and a red and blue pinstriped shirt.

Another doctor, who dressed a lot more civilized and looked to be in his late 50's, entered carrying an x-ray result taken from a CAT scan.

"Hi, Mister Maxwell."

"Call me Kirby."

"Okay, Kirby," the doctor obliged as he looked at Kathy. "I'm sorry, are you his wife? Please, don't get up."

"Yes, she's my wife," Kirby said. "Her name is Kathy."

"Well, my name is Doctor Lewis, Doctor Jonathan

Lewis. Kirby," the doctor said matter-of-factly. "I'm going to cut to the chase. You very nearly had a stroke. And you very well could have died from a brain aneurysm. Simply put, you were at death's door. I know it sounds scary, especially given your age, but it's true. You have to, I mean absolutely have to, slow yourself down. I don't know what your personal life is like, but, nevertheless, whatever it is, it's not worth you dying for. Slow down."

"Oh, my God," Kathy said.

"You should be pretty much out of danger now. We were able to drain most of the fluid out, but, you might feel woozy because you're sedated enough where you won't feel any pain. The rest of the rehabilitation process now begins with you."

"A stroke? How? Why? But..."

The doctor showed Kirby and Kathy the x-ray. He then asked Kirby if he ever remembered being struck on the head or in an accident where his neck or spine could have been injured. Kirby thought a moment, and then remembered when Shorty hit him in the head with the pool stick and threw him against a wall headfirst.

At that time was when the doctor provided Kathy and him with an explanation. The doctor cited although it was several years ago, the stress and strain he was going through caused fluid to build on the brain. Calcification, swelling on the brain, was the medical term he used. It happened in the spot where the skull was chipped by the blow he took. This was the reason for the blurred vision and migraines.

The news hit Kirby like a ton of bricks. He was grateful Junior sounded the alarm to Simon who then rushed him to the hospital.

Simon saved his life a second time, and he had not paid him back yet for the first.

The doctors left, but not before telling Kirby he would have to spend a few days and follow instructions. He agreed.

Kathy grabbed her saddened and teary-eyed husband by the hand and began rubbing it gently.

"Sweetie, why don't you come back home now," Kathy said as delicately as she knew how.

"Kathy..."

"We miss you so much. I miss you so much. You are my soul mate, Kirby and I love you."

"Kathy, I don't know about it right now. We argue too much. That's all we ever do—argue, argue, argue, fuss, fuss, fuss. I can't take the stress of it any more. I just can't."

"Who's gonna take care of you?"

"I'm not crippled. I'm not incapacitated. I'm just hurt, and I have to take it easy. I've been ready to leave IBM anyway. I'm ready to start my own consulting operation. I have enough money put away in case I have to take a loss for awhile. But, I have a lot of contacts, so it shouldn't be too long a wait."

"Kirby."

"Kathy, please," Kirby said and covered his eyes to

lessen the pain. He just did not want to talk about it any more.

Just as the conversation ended, Kirby's mother walked in.

"Son, Baby, are you alright? Baby, are you okay? What happened?"

"Yes, Momma, I'm fine. Momma calm down, I'm fine. I'm out of danger."

"What did they do to your head? What are all these bandages?"

"They..."

"Oh, Kathy, sugar, Momma's sorry. How are you?" Lois said and kissed her on the forehead.

"I'm fine, thank you."

"Tell me what's happening?" Lois demanded again and got the full explanation from Kathy.

Lois was pressed to the limit not to go over to Shorty's house, providing she could find it, and smash him about the head with an object.

Kirby urged his mother not to waste her time trying to look for him. Shorty, it was learned, was about to do time, five to ten, for armed robbery.

"Son, now I told you, you must take it easy. You can't save the world."

"Momma, I know. I'll take it easy."

"Promise me, Kirby," Lois said imploring him to respond with the answer she wanted to hear. "Promise me."

"I promise."

He Was My Hero, Too

"Say it again," Lois said as she looked him up and down. "And don't be trying to cross your fingers or your toes and all the other nonsense, either. I know your little tricks. I raised you, remember?"

"Yes Momma, I remember and I won't forget."

TWELVE

Kirby pressed the "off" button on his remote as he went to answer the knock on the door. It was Simon holding a large bag full of Chinese food.

"Smells good, man," Kirby said as he took the bag off Simon's hands and placed it on his kitchen table. "Whatcha got here?"

"Just a little egg fu young, General Tao's chicken, a little broccoli and rice, some spare ribs, some pork fried rice, and some moo goo guy pan."

"You got enough, Simon? Who are we feeding, Pharaoh's army?"

"Ay," Simon said and patted Kirby on the shoulder, before having a sit-down on the couch. "Whatever we don't eat, you keep."

Simon and Kirby chowed down and chatted easily, well into the wee hours of the night. Then the subject of Bennett came up.

"I still want to find Bennett's killer."

"Didn't the doctor tell you, you have to take things

easy. It's only been a week..."

Kirby gave Simon a look that made him hold his ears.

"Don't say it, my virgin ears can't take it."

"Oh stop it. What did Harry Hooch say?"

"Forget him for now, we have a meeting with Sol tomorrow at his office. I've been speaking with him off and on. He's talking about re-opening the case."

"Re-opening? It was never closed. It's still a cold case. Forget it..."

"I'll pick you up tomorrow morning at nine o'clock. Be dressed and ready to go. And if I have to drag you out of bed tomorrow, I will."

Tomorrow came but not a second too soon for Kirby; for he hated to see the man who married his deceased buddy's girlfriend. He was disapproving of the way it was done, but for Bennett's sake and not for his own, he willed himself into getting ready for the meeting. Besides, he felt himself grow queasy at the thought of Simon having to dress him.

He met Simon at the appointed time in front of his building, and the ride to City Hall was a breeze.

Outside, City Hall had this old-time colonial look to it and inside was made up of all marble and brass. It had a spiral staircase in the middle of it that led directly to the mayor's chambers. Simon and Kirby followed the stairway path as if they were being led to a slaughter.

When they reached the mayor's office, Kirby begrudgely asked the receptionist for Sol, to which

Simon had to elbow him.

"Come on Simon, it's not like I want to be here anyway."

"I know that, but he's our link right now."

Sol was expecting them, but they had to wait until Sol was done with his morning jog.

Before the two took their seats, Simon advised Kirby not to mention anything about Harry Hooch and his contacts.

Kirby hated being there but was quite impressed with the way Sol's digs looked.

It had a green thick rug that made one feel as if you were walking on air. The chairs were dark brown with thick seating and back leather padding on them. The huge maple wood desk had a sheet of glass covering it that made the place glisten with even more class. All of the pictures on the wall either were framed or laminated. The office also had a pine odor to it.

One half hour had passed when Sol would show. He had showered and changed his clothes beforehand.

"Gentlemen," Sol said as he walked in arrayed in a blue double-breasted suit, white shirt, and blue paisley tie. "How are you?" Sol was not only the first Jewish man elected to head the City of Mount Vernon; he was also, at age 31, the youngest.

Simon shook his hand immediately. Kirby reneged, leaving Sol hanging with his hand out. Simon again nudged him; this time with much more force.

"Yeah, how are you Sol, long time?"

He Was My Hero, Too

"I've been fine, and yourself?"

"Peachy...just dandy."

Simon shook his head and said to himself, 'you're gonna blow it Kirby. You're gonna blow it.'

"How's Tara?" Simon asked and received a dirty look from Kirby. Luckily Sol had bent down behind his desk for something or else he would have seen it and maybe changed his mind about helping them out.

"Fine, just fine. Matter-of-fact, she should be here any moment."

"She's coming here?" Kirby asked as unfriendly as possible.

"Yes. She'd like to see you. She hasn't seen you in almost ten years."

"Ten years too soon," Kirby mumbled.

"I'm sorry Kirby, did you say something?"

"No, I didn't say anything, I was just thinking out loud."

Sol and Simon began conversing about his mayorship, his family, and his future plans in politics. He had his eyes set on a down-the-line congressional or senatorial seat, a gubernatorial ticket, and eventually a presidential one.

The tête-à-tête was boring to Kirby, and he started to feel left out. He let out a loud sigh and Simon knew to change gears.

"Sol, we better get this ball rolling," Simon said in an attempt to calm Kirby down.

"Yes, yes of course," Sol said as he rambled through

some papers on his desk. "So you guys wish to re-open Bennett's murder case?"

"Re-open? Re-open? The case should never have been closed. The killer was never caught."

"I'm sorry Kirby, that's what I meant."

Just then, a knock on the door and an abrupt entrance was made. It was the very tall and slender, chief of police of Mount Vernon, Captain Floral Demetry Turner, the man with the whitest hair on the face of the earth. The man that had the nerve to one day try and dye it black, to which the nickname, "Captain Piano Head" was born.

He exchanged greetings with Simon and Kirby before making his way over to Sol to hand him a file folder and whisper in his ear.

He made his exit just that quickly. But, not before nodding his head at Simon and Kirby.

Kirby felt the whole shebang had gone wrong judging by the way Sol sat in his chair and fumbled with his pencil.

"Sol."

"His file is missing."

"I knew it was too good to be true. I knew something would go wrong," Kirby said and slapped on the arm of the chair. "Missing!"

"Yeah," Simon added. "Missing. I don't understand. You knew I, I mean we were coming. How could the files be missing?"

"As you know, the case was quite some time ago. I don't know, perhaps things were just transferred over somewhere without proper documentation to trace it. But, don't worry, I promise we'll find it. We will keep on top of it. It is a high priority matter."

Kirby had all he could stand and headed for the door. Simon had little choice but to follow suit. They came together; Simon lamented to himself, they must leave together.

"Wait fellas, please. I have good news. I mean really good news. You would want to hear this."

"You have a suspect?" Kirby said.

Sol propelled his way from behind his desk and made his way toward the door to meet with the two men. He then added, "No, it's not that."

"Well, what kind of good news would you possibly have at this point? Come on Sol, don't waste my time, and please don't toy with me."

"I assure you, I am not toying with you, Kirby. Trust me. Please sit and hear me out."

Kirby and Simon looked to one another to force an approval. Giving Sol the benefit of the doubt, they sat, not too trustfully, to hear what Sol had to say.

The news he had for them was Mount Vernon was planning to give Bennett a day.

The high school was going to induct Bennett into its Alumni Hall of Fame. And through donations and other sources, the high school was to have a scholarship in Bennett's name in the amount of $25,000. The award was to be given annually and dispersed among 100 students.

Sol also informed them that Fourth Street

Playground, as they presently knew it, would be, *The Bennett Wilson Memorial Playground*. And an annual basketball summer league will be held in his memory, and be dubbed, *the Bennett Wilson Memorial Open Invitational Tournament*.

The news brought a big smile to Kirby's face. He nearly jumped out of his seat. But that was not all, Sol had insisted. The playground, after a ground breaking and memorial ceremony, would be re-done with new tarp, new basketball goals, a new volleyball setup, and brand new plastic bleachers—something that would be able to withstand the constant change of the weather.

But the gem of them all, Sol added, would be something really special. Kirby and Simon thought, 'Wow, how more special can it get?'

Sol picked up a box and pulled out a bronze statue and handed it over to Kirby. Kirby was dumbfounded by it but was too excited about everything else to ask any questions.

Sol said he was going to finance the sculpturing of a ten-foot statue of Bennett to be placed directly in front of the high school. He said that Bennett would be holding books with his left hand. Under his right foot, he would be holding a basketball, and his right hand would point upward. Sol also added that words would be engraved on it. Something to the effect of, REACH HIGH, AIM HIGH, SOAR HIGH—THE SKY'S YOUR LIMIT. He felt those would be appropriate words coming from the mouth of Bennett and Kirby could not

He Was My Hero, Too

agree with him more as he beamed with excitement. He was so overcome with joy, he felt guilty for slugging Sol and smashing his glasses twelve years ago.

Sol gathered himself and told the two buddies everything would take place in June. The second week after school officially ends. It was a five-month wait and Kirby could hardly stand it.

"So how's Mrs. Wilson taking all of this?"

"Kirby, the woman cried for two days, she was so happy. She's still smiling, rightfully so, she deserves it. Bennett deserves it. Hey, Mount Vernon has got to honor our own. Bennett was then and still is an inspiration to us all. We've all learned something from him: courage, determination, and perseverance. Let's honor him."

"Sol, I'm sorry for everything I've done. I mean..."

"Ay, forget it," Sol said with a laugh.

Another greeter was at the door. This time the party waited for someone to ask who it was before entering.

It was Tara, and she was good and pregnant. The smile on Kirby's face had quickly vanished. His emotions were going crazy. He was ecstatic about Bennett's upcoming tributes, but seeing Bennett's ex pregnant by Sol seemed to bother him some.

Tara still looked the same as in high school. She was still fine. She had the same soft caramel complexion and those same chubby cheeks that dimpled whenever she smiled. Her body was a little—a lot disfigured, but it was to be expected given her condition.

"How are you Simon?" she said as she kissed him on

the cheek. "And how are you, Mister Kirby?" Tara's smile widened as she kissed Kirby also.

"I've been okay. How've you been?"

Kirby's stomach began to knot with anger as he watched Tara and Sol exchange kisses on the mouth. But he really got perturbed when he noticed Tara continuously pat on her belly while she tried to make conversation with them.

"How are Kitty Kat and the boys doing?"

"Everyone's fine, thanks. I'll tell them you sent your best."

"Please do so," Tara said as she sat down in an exhausted fashion. "Tell her, I'm going to be a mommy in two months, and I want her to come to my shower."

"Whoa, look at the time," Kirby said ending the conversation. "We better get outta here, Simon."

"Won't you guys stay for lunch?"

"Naw, we won't, Sol, sorry. But, we'll definitely keep in touch. If you find those files or if you guys come up with something, please inform me. I need to know. I still...you know."

"Yeah, I know," the two gentlemen shook hands. "I know."

Simon and Kirby were back in the hallway where it all started, not a moment too soon for Kirby's taste.

"Man, am I glad to be out of there. Where to now?"

Simon smiled and put his arm around his friend and led him down the steps, then added, "Next stop, the cemetery."

"Cemetery?"

"Yeah, I thought I told you it was Wanda's birthday, and I wanted to lay some flowers down for her."

"No, I don't recall. But I'll go. This way I can holler at Bennett and tell him the good news."

"Yeah," Simon said smiling, "I'm sure he'd like it."

The ride to the cemetery was quick. During the ride Kirby's thoughts were of Tara and her family of Sol and the upcoming baby. Kirby no doubt wished it were Bennett and Tara still together and having a baby. That of course would have meant Bennett would have still been alive.

Once they arrived at the cemetery, Kirby made his way over to where Bennett was laid to rest, while Simon went to where Wanda was. Simon knelt and placed a bushel of flowers down. He said a few words out loud to himself and then he began to pray. Suddenly, he heard the presence of a visitor. When he opened his eyes a shadow had engulfed him. Startled, he rose to his feet to see what or who it was towering over him.

"Can I help you, young man?" Simon asked.

"Who are you?" the rugged looking young man with the resonant voice asked.

"I'm Simon. Who are you?"

The young man then plucked out his toothpick and showed off his pearly whites mixed with gold and said, "I'm Wanda's younger brother, Wesley."

"Whoa, Wesley," Simon said and stuck out his hand. "Glad to meet you. I knew your sister."

"I know," Wesley said and squeezed Simon's hand so hard the blood had left it. Simon had to use his other hand to pry it away.

"I'm glad to finally meet you also. Finally," Wesley said and walked off whistling the melody of the Pink Panther cartoon.

Kirby approached Simon from behind as he watched Wesley stroll down the hill.

"Man, you scared me," Simon said as he continued to flex his hand trying to get the blood circulating in it again.

"Who was the man mountain?"

Simon hesitated before answering. The hesitation was so long, Kirby had to ask him a second time.

"Oh he, he, he was, is Wanda's brother. He said he was Wanda's brother."

Kirby saw the care-worn look on Simon's face, felt compassion for him, and asked him, "You nervous a little bit?"

"For some reason, I'm not just nervous. I'm a little frightened. Just a little though. But frightened, nonetheless."

"Don't worry, I got your back."

Simon displayed a fake smile and playfully slapped Kirby on the chest with his gloves, "Let's go see Harry Hooch."

THIRTEEN

"Harry Ho! Harry Ho! Harry Ho! Harry Hooch! Where you be, son? Come out! Come out! Wherever you are!" Simon yelled as he and Kirby walked up the squeaking steps of the dilapidated tenement building in the roughest section of Mount Vernon. The stairwell stunk something fierce. So much so, it took Kirby's breath away. Somehow Simon refused to mind. In fact, he seemed more inclined to wallow in it proclaiming, "Sol's office should smell this good."

"Shhh! Simon, come here," Harry Hooch said and motioned the two inside his cat-infested apartment.

"Look at all these cats," Kirby said as he dodged across the floor to keep from stepping on one.

"Don't worry, they're just here to keep me company and to keep the mice and roaches away."

"There's a better way," Simon chimed in and the two men hugged. "How you doing man?"

"I can't complain," Harry said as he took in another puff of his Winston-Salem. "Well, actually I can, but who would listen?"

Harry was a short, hairy, and scruffy looking man. He had so much hair on his body; it was close to impossible to determine his ethnicity. The hair on his head was jet black and long. He always donned a hat of some kind and dark shades, even while in-doors. He smoked cigarettes like they were going out of style, and his outward attire always had to have something with black in it. He was superstitious that way.

"I'll listen to you, Bra. You know you can count on me. Anytime."

Harry saw Kirby standing in the middle of the living room seemingly afraid to sit down.

"Have a seat, young man."

"No!" Kirby said as he looked down on the couch as if something was going to jump up and bite him. "I mean no, it's all right.

"Please, have a seat. This is my home."

"No, I don't think so."

"Kirby," Simon said with authority and in an attempt to defuse any tension that was in the offing.

"How many cats do you have, Hooch?" Kirby asked.

"Harry, call me Harry. And, I have nine cats."

Kirby, after sidestepping around and dodging cats in his path, was prompted to discontinue insulting Harry by Simon who this time let his eyes and body language do his talking.

"Where'd you find this guy, Simon?"

"He's a good guy. He's Bennett's best friend. He's the

He Was My Hero, Too

guy I was telling you about that wanted all of the information."

"Young fella," Harry Hooch said after taking a puff of his cancer-stick, "you married?"

Kirby somewhat taken aback by the question offered, "No, I'm not, but my wife is."

"Simon," a teed off Harry Hooch said. "Where'd you get this clown from?"

"Come on Hooch, everything's cool."

Kirby then inexplicably reached inside his pocket and pulled out a roll of $100 bills and handed them to Harry.

"What's this?"

"Your fee," Kirby said matter-of-factly.

Harry looked at Simon, and Simon looked at Kirby. No words were exchanged until Harry said to Simon, "You and I need to talk," and got up and went to a back room.

Simon went over to Kirby who wore a dumbfounded look on his face.

"What I do? What I say?"

"He doesn't take money until the job is complete. He thinks it's a jinx for him to get paid before hand."

"I don't know, Simon," Kirby said as he shook his head. "That guy's one weird bird. And, he's so hairy. He looks like a chia pet. Look...look at this nasty house. It looks like somebody's back yard. Grass! Dirt! At least I hope its dirt." Kirby said as he pointed at the brown substance at his feet.

"Ease up, man, relax. I think it's for the cats," Simon said and started for the back room as Harry called out again. "Anyway, I'll take care of everything. Why don't you help yourself to something in the fridge? Harry won't mind."

"You almost made me cuss. I don't care how much he gets insulted. I ain't eating or drinking nothing in here. The food would probably walk to me."

"Come on, Kirby…"

"Here, give him a breath mint."

"I'm coming, Harry! I'm coming!"

Kirby sat in absolute fear as the two men conferred in the back. He became even more terrified when three cats descended upon him. One went for his feet; one went for his head; and another jumped on his lap.

Kirby picked it up and threw it across the room. It landed safely on its feet.

Several minutes passed before the twosome at the end re-emerged. Harry made his way over to Kirby and stuck out his callous-ridden hand. Kirby looked at it carefully before relinquishing his. The two men shook hands and all was well again.

"Young fella, please forgive me. It's just I do business in a particular way, and sometimes it could lead to misunderstandings."

"Hey, I can dig it."

"Okay, now to the business at hand."

Harry went on about what he gathered through his own contacts.

He Was My Hero, Too

"Your friend, Bennett, was the victim of a hit. Someone put out a hit on him."

"What?" Kirby said, voice full of shock and amazement.

"Who paid the contract, I don't know. But, whoever did, had a lot of money. Either that or they had a lot of influence. The rifle used was no ordinary one.

"How do you know it was a rifle, I mean...?"

Harry looked at Simon, and Simon immediately tapped Kirby on the shoulder giving him the signal to shut up.

"I know by the bullet used. It was an assault rifle of some kind, and the barrel had been sawed off and switched. A common practice used by hitmen when they dealt with gunsmiths on the take.

But with all the information gathered, not finding out who the triggerman or money person behind it was was not the most puzzling issue. The fact someone wanted to kill Bennett in the matter in which he was killed, could not be answered. Aside from a little street skirmish and minor disagreements, having someone taken out in broad daylight like that was very disconcerting.

Harry, though, for all it was worth, vowed to get to the bottom of it. He believed he would come up with names, faces, and places within ample time. Usually, whenever Harry said something, he meant it.

Four hours came and went before Simon peeked at his watch and said, "Hooch, I'm outta here. I've got to go, now."

Simon noticed a mirthless look on Harry's hairy face.

"What's the matter? I'll keep in touch," Simon said with assuring laughter.

Harry's response prompted another voice of concern from Simon. This time it was with more sincerity.

"Hey Hooch, what's going on, man?"

"It's Little Tiny Smalls..."

"Oh yeah! How's my man doing?"

Harry Hooch began to shake his head in a negative fashion. "It doesn't look good for him. Not good at all. He really wants and needs to see you. He's in Bronx Lebanon Hospital."

"Hey Hooch, man, why didn't you tell me about this sooner? That's not right. You know how I feel about him. I love the guy..."

"He wants to see you so you can give him his last rites, Simon—you being the only preacher he really knows, let alone would trust. He wants you to come and give him his last rites."

"He's really that sick? What's wrong with him?"

"You'll have to see for yourself. Whatever it is though, it's got him. It's got him real good."

"Bronx Lebanon?"

"Yeah, he's in some special unit. You know, just ask for him, Lindsay Beale Donaldson, and they will direct you there. Take young fella, there, with you."

"Why?"

"Trust me, you'll want to take him with you."

He Was My Hero, Too

# # #

"Hi, I'd like to see Mister Lindsay Beale Donaldson," Kirby said to the receptionist as he stood in the lobby of the Bronx Lebanon Hospital.

The hospital was unlike the one in Mount Vernon. The people were not nearly as friendly, and the whole place seemed to be unkempt. It was more like patients went there to die rather than to be cured.

"Oh, here he is, Unit 4A. You'll have to take these visitors' passes, please."

"Thank you. Here, Kirby, yours."

As Simon and Kirby strolled down the corridor en route to Little Tiny's room, all they could hear were sighs of agony coming from patients. Patients squealed as if being pierced with a sharpened object.

They reached Tiny's room and a look of gloom splattered upon Simon's face. He saw Little Tiny Smalls.

"Tiny?" Simon said, looking for a little assurance.

He remembered Harry Hooch telling him how sick he was, but hearing how much his looks had changed was not the same as seeing it for himself.

Tiny, who once carried well over 300 pounds, was hovering around 90 pounds and looked very weak. The black hair that once topped his skull had all of a sudden turned off-white and was reduced to spots and patches. The massive hands he used to have were small and frail looking. His fingernails were jet black. Mostly every tooth was missing. Those that remained were rotten to the core.

Kirby's head began to hurt, as he had to take a seat in the hall.

"Simon, my friend, you came to see about me?" Tiny said. You could tell every breath became an ordeal for the man who at one time was known to have the strength of Samson.

"Yeah, man. I would've come sooner if only I had known."

"You came at the right time, believe me. I'm so glad to see you. I see you have your young fella taggin' along with you."

"We were taking care of some business, together. How are you feeling?"

Tiny, who was hooked up to an intravenous feeder, began coughing uncontrollably as he hacked up blood. This sight frightened Simon terribly.

"You want me to get the nurse?"

"No, no, this happens all the time. I'm used to it."

Simon started wiping Tiny's face with a towel when a nurse entered and stated, "You're not supposed to handle the patients without gloves on."

"What?"

"Hospital rules, sir...I'm sorry sir."

"Rules? This is my friend. I'm not going to handle him with gloves. I'm not. I refuse."

"I'm sorry sir," the pudgy nurse with the red hair and freckles said as she handed Simon a pair of gloves.

The two talked a while as Simon managed to become more comfortable with Tiny's condition. Reminiscing on old times seemed to put a smile on Tiny's face. But Tiny looked to be getting weary and Simon sensed it, "I better be going now. I'll see you real soon...probably Saturday."

"No, Simon, you won't see me on Saturday."

"Why," Simon said trying to give Tiny hope. "You leaving to go home? Is this place a place where I won't find you? Harry Hooch will find you for me."

Tiny smiled a bit and stuck his hand out. Simon was reluctant to grab it for fear he might hurt him.

"Simon, I have AIDS and I don't think I'll make it to Saturday. Simon, I'm dying. I'm a dead man."

Tears of sorrow forced their way out of Simon's eyes and trickled down his face. Kirby looked in through the glass window and saw him sobbing and made his way back inside.

"Hey young fella, how you doin'?"

"I'm fine, Tiny. I'm just fine."

"I'm cool, Kirby, wait for me outside. Thanks."

"You sure? Okay then, but I think I'll go down to the lobby and wait. Tiny, you take care of yourself and get well soon."

"Take care of yourself, young fella. Be good."

Simon tried to regain his composure so he would be able to speak intelligently. It was hard, but he managed.

"What do you mean, you have AIDS? You didn't go that way. I don't..."

"I was messing with one of my girls, she was infected. She was an IV drugger." Tiny said, as his eyes became blood shot as the pain seeped through his fragile body.

"Oh Tiny," Simon said as tears began to flow again. "You knew the rules. We never mixed business with pleasure, let alone not wearing a raincoat. Tiny, this is the mid-eighties, we knew this from the beginning of time."

Tiny's cough came back again and blood, saliva, and mucus accompanied it. Simon did as he had done so before and helped his friend out.

"I know, but I took a liking to her."

"Is she still alive?"

"She died two years ago, not long after Big Willie passed. But, she wasn't the only one I was with, so I don't know."

Tiny spoke some more about his condition, and afterward, he pointed to his right arm.

"No Tiny, you shot up to? Were you trying to kill yourself, man?"

"No, Simon, I got reckless, and I got careless, that's all. I just got careless, and I didn't protect myself. And I'm going to die for it." Tiny's conversation was again interrupted with another series of whooping coughs accompanied by blood, saliva, and mucus. "Warn those kids you love so much. Warn them and use me for an example. Warn them." Tiny took some time to suck in some air, then added, "Simon, I can't fight this. I can't fight this even with my stick."

The last remark garnered a slight smile from Simon.

"I don't know what to do, Tiny."

"I want you to give me my last rites. I'm sure Hooch told you."

"Let's pray for healing instead."

"Simon, I wish I could. But I don't have the faith. I'm weak. My spirit is broken. If you love me, you'll do it for me."

"Tiny..."

"Don't ask God to forgive me. I've already done it a thousand times over."

"What do you want me to pray for?"

"Ask God to take care of my family: My brother and sister and their kids. Ask him to bless them and continue to look over them. They're good people."

"Okay," Simon said and tapped Tiny's chest.

"But most of all," Tiny said as he sat back and allowed tears to run down his face. "Please, Simon, ask God to have mercy on my soul. Ask him to have mercy on my soul. Ask him, if He will, to receive my spirit and bless me. As my friend and brother, I want you to give me my last rites."

"Tiny..."

"I feel death comin' for me soon, Simon. I can hear the chariots comin' for me now. I'll be dead before you get home tonight. I know it. I'll be gone."

"Tiny, I love you," Simon said as he placed his hand on his buddy's forehead. "Close your eyes, let's pray."

FOURTEEN

"Three weeks elapsed and Simon eulogized his good friend Tiny and buried him, all at his own expense. Normally, not rain, sleet, nor snow would prevent Simon from having his "Brotherhood Night," Even if just but one person showed, "Brotherhood Night" would still go on.

But there was an exception to this rule. Simon was tormented by the cause of Tiny's death. And with the plea from him to warn the kids of the potential danger of it happening to them. Simon was determined to go all out with his next lecture. He would spend two weeks promoting the effort. He went on local radio shows. He bought advertising space in the local papers, and he was also on a few of the cable outlet programs.

The response was tremendous. Mount Vernon High School offered its gymnasium. Simon was grateful, but he refused, citing the boy's club was where it all started and was where he would prefer to have it.

Simon wanted young ladies present at this particular

He Was My Hero, Too

event. He wanted successful and serious career-minded and health-conscious women to act as keynote speakers or support people.

His wife, LoNelle, being a registered nurse and all, was to be a keynote speaker on behalf of the females in attendance.

"This is serious to me, very serious," Simon said to Kirby while sitting behind his desk, lurking in and out of deep thought.

"What are you talking about, 'Brotherhood Night'?"

"Yeah, I've never been as nervous or as intense as I am now. I don't know what it is."

"It's the subject matter, AIDS. It's out there. Big time."

"Man, I've been in prayer all week."

"Is that anything unusual for you?" Kirby asked playfully trying to relax Simon.

"No," Simon said lightheartedly. "I guess it's not. I guess I should just calm down some."

"I think that's a good idea."

Wednesday night would at last dawn and the sun could not set a moment too soon. A multitude of locals and visitors made their way inside the boys' club. To help accommodate the overflowing crowd, extra bleachers were brought in as well as fold-up chairs and benches. The other rooms of the club were rigged with speakers for those not able to make it inside the gym.

Simon sat on the panel with LoNelle, Billy Thomas, James Jones, Lowes Moore, and a doctor, who was a good friend and colleague of LoNelle's.

A green chalkboard with wheels was setup and decorated with prophylactics as well as female birth control devices. Also propped against the chalkboard was a broom, which seemed out of place.

Simon wore a very stern expression as he walked to the podium. It did not look like there would be any jokes told after this lecture was over. But only time would tell.

"Good evening, ladies and gentlemen, boys and girls."

"Good evening, Bra Simon," was the response returned from the enormous crowd.

"We all know why we're here," Simon said in a sullen voice as he played with the change in his pocket. "Because it's 'Brotherhood Night', that's why we're gathering here. Usually, as you all know, this night is reserved for young men. Or I should say, males. And there are times when women infiltrate the meetings. I never really minded. But this night is different. I wanted you...females to be here. Thank you for coming." The last remark was received with a round of applause.

"My wife, LoNelle, will get the chance to speak on behalf of the women and young ladies in attendance. But we should all stay and hear her, for it affects both men and women.

The issue I'll be speaking to you about is human relations...sex." Simon went over to the chalkboard and picked up the broom. "I want you guys to understand this. I am not encouraging you, especially, you minors in here, to have sex, particularly if you're not married and monogamous. But if it did happen, please, please, please protect yourself. There's a disease called AIDS out there that will kill you dead if you come in contact with it. And from what I found out, you don't have to be homosexual and an IV drug user to get it. And the doctor here," Simon said and slapped his thigh. "I'm sorry, please welcome Doctor Richard Evans—he will explain about it further. Many of you—Mount Vernonites— either knew or probably heard of Little Tiny Smalls, well, he died from AIDS. He suffered first, and then he died. I don't want that to happen to you, any of you."

Simon went on at great lengths about his experience with Tiny and again encouraged those under the sound of his voice to protect themselves rather than wreck-themselves. He, along with the doctor, gave a demonstration of how to properly use a condom. Graphic and explicit detail on how body fluids travel and interact causing infection was not withheld. There were quite a few "ooohs" and "ahhhs" heard throughout the demonstration, all to which, Simon took comfort in. For he felt his words were getting through, being absorbed, and not just falling on deaf ears. They also noted that condoms and the other forms of protection were not fool proof. The safest way to protect yourself against disease and unwanted pregnancy was abstinence.

Simon then gave the floor to LoNelle, and she took the baton from there. LoNelle was more into preventing pregnancy, other STD's and hygiene issues. The focus of her speech centered on women showing respect for themselves, to be more lady-like, despite their needs.

The night of lectures once again ended. But the crowd seemed to want more information. Very few left before the panel had their time at the microphone.

Simon, in conclusion, lightened up enough—with the constant urging of the crowd—to tell one of his trademark jokes.

"Okay, okay, one quick one," Simon acquiesced. "A man is sitting at the bar of a local speakeasy. And after every shot of whiskey, he looked into his shirt pocket and then instinctively ordered another drink. He repeated the process again and again. This goes on for about eight or nine times, when at last the bartender asked him, 'Man, why do you always look inside your shirt pocket after you finish a drink?' The man looked up at him and winced. 'In my pocket here is a picture of my wife. And whenever she starts to look good to me, I'll go home.'"

The whole places, gymnasium, extra rooms, and even the overflow outside exploded with laughter. With such a tension-filled lecture program, the joke was obviously well timed and welcomed.

"Great speech," Wanda's brother Wesley said as he grabbed Simon's hand and clenched it really tight.

"Thanks, I'm glad you enjoyed it," Simon said and yanked his hand back.

Wesley then gave Simon a menacing smile and walked away.

"Man," Kirby said as he made his way into Simon's office. "You were great. So were the rest of the folk up there. Everybody was on point."

"Thanks," Simon said as he took off his drenched suit jacket and placed it behind his chair. "What's that you have there?"

"Oh, this?" Kirby asked as he lifted a "Gatsby's Men's Clothing" garment bag. "This is a new suit I bought. I have a big day tomorrow."

"What's so big about tomorrow?"

"Well, first off, I have a meeting with a potential client, in New Rochelle."

"Get outta here. Already?"

"Yeah, man," Kirby said and took a seat. "I can't take too much time off. I'll get bored. Then my head will really start bothering me."

"Don't work yourself too hard. One reason why you're not at IBM is because of your head. Take it easy. The fainting spell wasn't too long ago."

"And," Kirby said with a wily smile, swiftly changed the subject.

"There's more?"

"I have a little dinner date with Kat, tomorrow night."

Simon looked up to the ceiling and screamed, "Hallelujah," then got up and grabbed Kirby and gave him a bear hug.

"Man, I told you, you guys would get back together."

"Whoa Simon, it's just dinner. Just dinner."

"It's a date, right?"

"Yeah, I guess you could say that. But..."

"That's all I needed to know. My prayers have been answered. Oh, man, have a great time."

"Thanks, but what are you doing tomorrow?"

"I have a few errands to run in the morning, and I'm supposed to meet with Sol in the evening."

"What for? Did he locate the missing files?"

"To be honest, he didn't. But we are to go over some plans regarding 'Bennett Wilson Day.' "

"What's going on?"

"City Hall and the high school are trying to see if they can do everything in one day. They feel it will have a greater impact."

"Sounds good, but it sounds like an all-day thing to me."

"Exactly," Simon said and sat back down. "Hey, get on out of here. Go home and get some rest. I don't want you tired on your big day tomorrow."

"I am tired," Kirby said as the two men shook hands. "I'll call you tomorrow night."

"I hope you're not in a position to be able to. If you know what I mean." Simon said, then gave Kirby a wink and a smile.

"Yeah, I know what you mean. I know exactly what you mean."

# # #

Kirby went home and slept not a wink. He bubbled

He Was My Hero, Too

with excitement well into the wee hours. The thought of his first independent client meeting was enough to make him feel geeky. But his date with Kathy since their two-year detachment was enough to make him want to do cartwheels.

The next morning Kirby got up, showered, and shaved. His nerves were so upset; he forewent breakfast, which is something he never does. But before going to his 11 o'clock meeting, he made a quick stop at a florist. He had two-dozen long-stem roses delivered to Kathy at her job.

The meeting went extremely well with Kirby and his potential client. In fact, it had gone even better than Kirby expected. The man hired Kirby to set up his computer operation for his new clothing outlet.

With the day starting off on a good note, Kirby was optimistic that the night with Kathy would turn out just as good if not better. His next destination would be his favorite barber shop in New Rochelle—Big 3 Hair Shop on Main Street—this, after he bit down on a hot-dog from Nathan's.

He got his hair buffed just the way he liked it. His barber, Dale Green, always knew just what to do. Now it was off to White Plains again. This time to freshen up, change his shirt and tie, and put on a fresh coat of Kathy's favorite cologne, Polo, by Ralph Lauren. His brand new suit looked just fine on him, as he modeled before the mirror at least a dozen times.

Now it was off to Metro North to catch an express

train into New York City, for he and Kathy were to wine and dine at Central Park's Tavern on the Green. Kathy would meet him there, for she worked for a brokerage firm in midtown Manhattan.

The ride was swift and smooth, and Kirby got off at the last stop—Grand Central Station. He was sky high and unable to contain himself, so he decided to jog the twenty-nine blocks as opposed to taking a cab.

Fifteen

"Simon, where've you been?" Harry Hooch said over the telephone. "Did you get my message? I've been looking all over for you."

"I just called LoNelle. She gave me the message to call you. What's up, you sound nervous."

"I am. I've got some heavy news for you about Bennett's killer. I'm talking suspects, names, places, and reasons. This is really, really, heavy. Where are you calling me from, anyway? You at the club?"

"No, I'm at City Hall, the mayor's office with Sol."

"You, what?"

"What's wrong Hooch?"

"Nothing, nothing, I need you to meet me somewhere."

"Calm down, Hooch, I'll meet you. Where?"

"Meet me at the abandoned brick warehouse on Third Avenue behind the Salvation Army, in two hours. It'll take me a little while to get back uptown. We should be alone there. It's deserted that time of night."

"Okay, Hooch, two hours, let me run."

"Hey, don't mention…" the telephone clicked. "Simon! Simon!"

# # #

When Kirby arrived, Kathy had already beaten him there, and she was seated at a table. Kirby spotted her across the room of the lavishly furnished posh restaurant with the help of the man offering hospitality. She was sipping on a glass of water. Kathy was decorated in her favorite blue dress, her hair appeared to be recently done, it was shoulder length—just the way Kirby liked it—and she wore the pearl earrings and necklace set he had bought for a previous Christmas. One could tell she shared the same excitement as Kirby.

"Hi, Kat," Kirby said as the once happy man and wife couple exchanged handshakes and kisses at the same time. "Good to see you. You look fantastic. Man, you look good." Kathy blushed then burst out into a soft chuckle.

"May I get you something?" the host clad in black and white offered.

"Yes, we'll have one of your house appetizers. I don't care," Kirby said as he put a tip into the fellow's hand without looking at him. His eyes were fixated on Kathy.

"Wow Kathy," Kirby said and sat down. "You really look…good!"

"Kirby, stop…you're embarrassing me. Besides," Kathy said and licked her lips seductively. "You don't look half bad yourself. In fact, you look good enough to eat."

The gesture and statement almost made Kirby choke on his water.

"You hungry, Kat?" Kirby said as he picked up the menu.

"Pretty much," Kathy said and picked up her own menu. "I haven't eaten anything all day."

"Me either. I just had a hotdog. But it almost took me an hour to eat it."

"Kirby, you know you have to eat. You have to take medicine."

"Yes, Mother."

The waiter delivered the appetizers of fried shrimp and took their orders. And in a matter of minutes, the main course had come and gone.

The offer of dessert was declined, but Kirby and Kathy stayed a while to chat.

"Kirby," Kathy said innocently. "What happened to us? What went wrong?"

Kirby took time to carefully configure his words before speaking. He knew how important the question was. Not just for a possible reconciliation but for the mental and emotional psyche as well.

"Kat," Kirby said as he folded his arms, "the best thing I could come up with is that we married too young. I don't know if it's excusable but that's how I feel. Nobody forced us to do it. We did it because we wanted to."

"Kirby, I married you straight out of high school because I fell deeply in love with you and I wanted to spend the rest of my life with you. I wanted to have your children. I was determined to make it work and to also make a life for myself. When you went away and joined the Navy and I got pregnant with Junior, I was determined I would still go to college and get my degree. And when you left the Navy and enrolled in that two year computer school, I maintained everything around the house, didn't I?"

"Yes, and you did a great job. I've always said..."

"Because to get what we both wanted out of life, I knew it would take two of us at least having decent jobs, to help the family prosper. I had Bennie, during my junior year of college, but I didn't miss a beat. I'm a CPA now. I have a great job. You have a great job."

"Well," Kirby corrected. "I had one."

"You know what I mean. And you know, IBM would take you back in a flash. It's up to you and how you're feeling, health-wise."

"Oh, Kathy," Kirby said with a trace of excitement in his voice. "I landed my first client today."

"That's great..."

"So I doubt if I'll go back to IBM anytime soon. Not if I can work at my own leisure or pace and still make good money."

Kathy shook her head in awe and thought of how proud she was of the man she once considered to be her soul mate. Then she offered, "How's your head? Are you still having pain?"

"No, not really. My head is fine: no stress, no tension, and no real aggravation. I'm feeling pretty good."

Kathy felt the comment was indirectly related to her and asked, "Kirby, are you calling me aggravating?"

"Kat, where'd that come from? I was referring to my work, not you."

"So what happened to us?" Kathy asked.

"We just grew apart, that's all. With your job and mine, I think we stopped doing the things we used to do and got comfortable doing that."

Kathy let out a deep and long sigh before adding, "I hope that...oh nothing."

Kirby had started trying to make Kathy laugh. He was saying crazy things, making faces, and bopping his head back and forth. His attempt was met with huge success as Kathy started crying tears of laughter.

"Boy," she said as she dotted her eyes. "I really miss you acting silly like Bill Cosby."

Kirby smiled sheepishly and said, "Is that all you miss?"

"Kirby, we're in a restaurant," Kathy said and laughed again, this time with a little more giggle to it.

"Hey, we're married. And the Bible states," Kirby started pointing his index finger mimicking a preacher they both knew, "the bedroom in marriage should not be defiled."

Kathy again followed form and laughed at a Kirby statement. Then she added her little two cents, "It figures."

"What?"

"Here it is, you go to church maybe four times a year but you know everything about the Bible that pertains to..." Kathy stooped her head over and said in a very light whisper, "sex."

"Sex!"

"Shhh, lower it down. You are a nut. Like I said," Kathy continued in a whisper, "if it has something or anything to do with marital relations, you master it."

"Hey, I gotta start somewhere, don't I?"

Kathy waved her hand at him and again laughed some more. The mood quickly turned as Kathy stared intensely at Kirby.

"What's wrong, Kat?"

Her eyes began to fill up with water.

"I miss you, Kirby. I want you to come home. I want my husband back. The kids miss you something terrible."

"But, I..."

"I know what you're gonna say. You spend time with them. And you do. I think you're a great father. You really are wonderful with them. But, Honey, I miss you and I want you back."

Kirby blushed a little, sipped on his warm glass of water, and then said, "Kat, I miss you too. I miss my family too. I still love you. I still love you very much. I never stopped."

"Well," Kathy said.

"Um...the lease is up in my apartment in two weeks.

So, I'll come home. I'm ready for us to be a family again. I'm ready."

"Yes! Thank you God!" Kathy said and jumped over to the other side of the table to kiss on her "new" husband.

"Kat," Kirby tried to say in between smooches, "don't forget, we're in a restaurant, remember?"

"Oh yeah, I almost forgot," Kathy said with her laugh coming back to her. She got off Kirby's lap as patrons began staring, and took her seat again. "Baby, we'll make this work. We'll do..."

Before Kathy could go on about all she thought could, should, and would take place, Kirby quickly countered, "Let's just take one day at a time. Believe me, I'm just as happy about this as you are. But...you know. One day at a time."

"Okay, I can handle it. I'm still going to be excited though."

"So, Kat," Kirby said with a mischievous look. "When do we consummate this thing? I mean, when are you gonna hit me off?"

"Why didn't I know that was coming?"

"Hey, I'm just following procedure here. You know," Kirby started rolling his hands. "I'm just following tradition, that's all."

"That's all, huh? Well, I would love to tonight but..."

"Aw, don't tell me it's that time..."

"No, silly," Kathy said as she looked at her watch. "After ten years of being together and nine years of marriage, you should know that by now. I'm like clockwork, remember? You used to say it all the time."

"Yeah, yeah, but what's the problem then?"

"It's the kids. I promised Zora I'd pick them up by ten. And it's close to that now. How're we getting home, Kirby?"

"We'll catch a cab," Kirby said then inquired one last time. "But can't we...?"

"She has an early day tomorrow. Otherwise, I would. How about tomorrow? Tomorrow, I'll get my mother to watch them. They can spend the night with her. And you can come over or I'll come to your place," Kathy laughed again.

"What's so funny? This ain't no laughing matter now, Kat. This is serious. I mean real serious. That's probably why my head was hurting."

"Well, I'm laughing because I'm happy. And secondly, I'm laughing because I don't believe I'm sitting here trying to arrange a tryst with my own husband."

"What do you prefer, it be someone else?"

"No, crazy. It's usually...forget it, let's go. I love you."

"I love you too, Kat."

SIXTEEN

"Harry Ho! Harry Ho! Harry Ho! Harry Hooch! Where you be, son? Come out! Come out! Wherever you are!"

A man's shadow appeared from the dimness of light, but the shadow did not resemble Harry's build. Simon became nervous and picked up a steel pipe he spotted on the floor.

"Man, what are you doing here?" A somewhat relieved Simon asked. The person did not answer. A gun was drawn toward him and the chamber was cocked.

"What's the business with the gun?" a now incredulous Simon asked.

Again the person did not answer.

"What are you doing? And, where's Harry? Harry," Simon yelled out, "you all right?"

"Save your breath, he's dead. He's back to the dirt from whence he came. And you are about to join him."

"What? What are you talking about?"

"I'm talking about putting your lights out, permanently."

Simon became unraveled. "Wait a minute. Please, oh please don't..." Simon said as he slowly backed away.

"It's too late," the gunman said shaking his head, "way, way too late."

"Listen," Simon said as he began to sweat profusely, "I don't want to die. Please don't kill me."

"Why shouldn't I?"

"Man, please don't shoot me. Please," Simon begged and pleaded for his life.

"I always wanted to see you sweat," the gunman said, smiling.

"You got it, you got it, now please let me live. Let's talk about this. Please don't kill me."

"I asked you before, why shouldn't I?" the gunman asked defiantly. "You're out there snooping around in my business. I don't like that. You wouldn't let sleeping dogs lie. You just wouldn't! You keep nosing around!"

"Man...please don't," Simon pleaded again.

"Shut up! Just shut up! You talk too much! Shut up! And stop whining!"

"Okay, okay," Simon said and backed further away. The pipe was still in his hand.

The gunman was suddenly distracted by a loud noise. Simon thought fast and seized the opportunity to charge after him. As Simon drew closer, the gunman regained his poise and whacked Simon across the face with his backhand. Simon tumbled backwards and landed between two huge boxes.

He Was My Hero, Too

The gunman slowly walked and stood over a dazed Simon. "Good-bye," he said and smiled menacingly.

Seventeen

Kirby reached his own home after dropping Kathy off and sharing a long kiss like the old days.

As usual, the first person he would see as he entered the lobby would be the concierge, Antonio.

"My friend, how are you on this evening?"

"I'm feeling just great," Kirby said and gave him a tip.

"Why such big smile? You get lucky in love?"

"Yes," Kirby said with his smile beaming even more. "I'm getting back with my wife, Kathy."

"Oh, so that's why so sad, you and wife separate. Me and wife together, 4 children 37 years."

"Wow 37 years, that's good, I mean great."

"When you go back?"

"My lease is up at the end of the month, and I'll just not renew it and move out."

"Me," Antonio, with the heavy Italian accent said, "I retire in six months. Be finish."

"Congratulations," Kirby said and shook Antonio's

He Was My Hero, Too

hand.

"You have quarter?"

"I just gave you a tip."

"No, no," Antonio said as he held up his two hands. "No tip. Take quarter out of pocket."

Kirby shook his head because he did not know what was happening but reached inside his pocket and took one out nonetheless.

"What year quarter?"

Kirby turned the quarter over and answered, "1984."

"Eighty-four," Antonio said and reached inside of his pocket. From the sound of things, one could have thought Antonio was carrying at least ten extra pounds just from coins. "I have eighty-four also."

"Okay?"

"Let's change."

"Huh?"

"You...me switch quarter." Antonio said and snatched Kirby's away from him. "Here, take mine and put in wallet. Never spend, keep forever. I keep yours in wallet. Never spend, keep forever. Whenever I see quarter, I think of you. Never forget."

"Okay...that'll work. Friends forever, I like that," Kirby said and shoved the quarter into a compartment inside of his wallet.

The two men hugged as Antonio grabbed the unsuspecting Kirby. "I'll miss you, my friend. I'll miss very much my friend, forever."

"Take good care of yourself, Antonio."

Before he knew it, Kirby was back upstairs. He was so excited about going home again; he started packing his clothes. When he was just about to turn in for the evening, he was interrupted with a phone call.

"LoNelle?" Kirby asked. "What's wrong?"

"It's Simon, he's not home yet, and it's well past 2:00 A.M. I'm worried. He'd never stay out this late without calling," she spitted out.

"Doesn't sound like him. Doesn't sound like him at all."

"I'm sorry for calling you this late."

"Please, LoNelle," Kirby said as he searched around for his shoes, "I'd be angry if you hadn't. It's not a problem. Did he say where he was going last?"

"I know he told me he had to meet with the Harry Hooch, guy."

"Oh, you mean Hairy Hooch?"

LoNelle was able to force out a slight laugh before she answered, "Yeah, him. He said Harry had some serious information to give him. I didn't ask him what it was, but it sounded really important. Maybe I'm just a little paranoid. Maybe they're just out having a good time, and he lost track of the time. But I'm worried Kirby, I'm worried."

"That's okay, I am as well," Kirby said as he re-snapped his pants. "But, did Simon say or give a hint to where he was going to meet him? And where was he when you last spoke?"

"When he called me last, he was at the mayor's

He Was My Hero, Too

office," LoNelle said. She then paused for a moment to think and get her bearings. "I believe I heard him say something about the Salvation Army. I don't know if it makes any sense or not."

Kirby took a moment to think before repeating, "Salvation Army, Salvation Army—Third Avenue—warehouse. Did he say something about a warehouse?"

"It sounds..."

"LoNelle, I'll call you back when I find him. Just sit tight."

Kirby hung up the phone, snatched on his suit jacket, and headed out the door for his car. He must have shattered every speed law on the Hutchinson Parkway and ran every red light from White Plains to Mount Vernon. The good Lord was with him, no cops were around at the time of his Mario Andretti impersonation.

Kirby arrived at his destination and noticed Simon's car amidst the darkness and fog. He began to get nervous as he picked up a brick and headed toward the building. He jumped in fear as a black cat whisked past him.

"Simon! Simon! Can you hear me? Are you there?"

Kirby walked around some more until he noticed a foul smell in the air. He looked down and saw Harry bleeding about the head with his eyes bugged open.

"Harry! Oh no! Oh no! What in the world!" Kirby said and reached down. Kirby took his hand and pressed Harry's neck to see if he were still alive. There was no pulse. Harry was dead.

"I gotta find Simon," Kirby jumped up clutching the brick by his side. He was determined to find his friend. If only he could call LoNelle and tell her Simon was all right, that he had found him. Kirby made it inside the warehouse and started running.

Kirby's sprint was interrupted when he lost his footing on something slippery. He went two feet in the air and landed on the ground, causing the brick to fly out of his hand. Kirby, slightly dazed, got up and looked around to see what he tripped on. He was unable to distinguish what it was, for the darkness was too great. He took a few steps forward and tripped again. This time it was a hat. After Kirby picked it up and examined it, that is when he heard the sound of a person moaning in agony and noticed Simon lying on the ground.

"Simon!" Kirby said as he knelt to him. "You all right? Please be all right! Please!"

There was no answer from Simon as he bled from his chest and shoulder. Kirby cradled him in his arms as he felt for a pulse.

"Bennett, who, oh God, I mean Simon, who did this to you?"

Kirby's head throbbed from seeing his good friend covered in blood.

"Simon, don't die on me, man. Keep your eyes open. Man, fight back! Simon! You better not die on me." Kirby instinctively started seeking for help he knew was not there. He then felt his chest and stomach area and noticed how drenched his shirt became. "Man,"

Kirby said still touching himself, "you're bleeding all over my brand new suit. Fight, man!"

Simon's body temperature dropped and his teeth started to chatter.

"Oh God, please don't let him die now," Kirby pleaded. "He has a family; a wife and a little girl. Please!"

Kirby began to cry and cradle Simon tighter.

"Yeah Simon, keep your eyes open," Kirby said as he rocked back and forth.

Kirby's mind was racing a mile a minute. He thought of all types of ways to try to calm Simon and himself down. After a while something finally came to him. "I-I-I-I, have a joke for you. Simon, come on, man listen to me. Keep your eyes open. Listen to this…a bride and groom was at rehearsal for their wedding. During the rehearsal, the groom secretly approached the pastor with an unusual offer: 'Look,' he said, 'I'll give you $100 bucks if you'll change the wedding vows up some. When you get to the part where I'm supposed to promise to love, honor and obey and be faithful to her forever. I'd appreciate it very much if you'd just leave that out.' He then passed the minister a $100 bill and walked away satisfied. On the day of the wedding, when it came time for the groom's vows to be said, the pastor looked the young man in the eye and said, 'Will you promise to prostrate yourself before her, obey her every command, wish and desire? Will you promise to serve her breakfast in bed every morning of your life, and swear eternally before the church and your lovely wife that you will never even look at another woman, as long as you live?' The groom smiled sheepishly, gulped and looked around. Then he said in a tiny voice, 'yes,' and leaned toward the pastor and hissed, 'I thought we had a deal, man. What's up?' The pastor smiled and winked at the young lad. He then put a $100 bill into his hand and whispered, 'She made me a better offer.'"

Simon through the midst of all his agony managed a feeble smile.

"Come on, Simon, keep your eyes open." Kirby said as he saw Simon's eyes roll back in his head. "Oh God please!" Kirby screamed. He then placed Simon down, ripped off his jacket and laid it under Simon's head. He took off his shirt and put it under Simon's left shoulder.

"You're scaring me," Kirby said as he saw Simon's eyes roll back once again. "Don't leave me, man. Please don't leave."

Kirby got up and looked around again. He spotted a ray of light. He figured it was an entranceway so he made a break for it. "Help! Help! Help! Somebody! Somebody shot Simon! Help! Somebody call an ambulance! Please! Somebody Help! Somebody call for help! Please!"

THE END

ABOUT THE AUTHOR

Jerald Levon Hoover was born December 3, 1965, in New York City. Jerald is an award-winning author. This is his second novel (a sequel to *My Friend, My Hero*) and part two of a four-book, *"Hero Series."* He is an avid sports fan, who also enjoys traveling, and reading. Jerald is a musician and Sunday school teacher. He is also a member of Concerned Black Men, where he serves as a mentor in the public schools and the community. Jerald is also a 1998 inductee of the South-side Mount Vernon Boys and Girls Club Hall-of-Fame.

You can contact Jerald Hoover at:
www.JeraldHoover.com or JLHproductions@aol.com
You can also email him at Hoover1216@aol.com.

TOPICS OF DISCUSSION

1. The importance of a good relationship between PARENT and CHILD.
2. The importance of FAIR play. Going through life without having to cheat.
3. Saying "NO" to drugs.
4. Saying "NO" to alcohol.
5. Saying "NO" to guns.
6. The importance of having the RIGHT kind of friends.
7. The ability to realize that you are you own person, and not let peer pressure become an endangerment to you.
8. Make everyday count toward working at a positive goal.
9. The importance of staying in school.
10. The significance of striving to avoid unplanned teen-age pregnancy.

ESSAY QUESTIONS

1. a) Who do you think shot Bennett?
   b) And is it still important?
2. Imagine you are Kirby, how do you feel - about your life, now and then?
3. a) Should women be excluded from the men's meetings?
   b) Why?
4. a) This should be a well-known fact by now, but what do the letters A.I.D.S mean?
   b) How can it affect the life of an individual?
4. Did it change the way Simon felt towards his friend, Little Tiny Smalls?
6. In what way did Bennett's little brother Dannon remind everyone of him?
7. Do you think Kirby and Simon were truly friends?
8. a) What landed Simon in prison?
   b) Do you think it did him any good?
9. How did Kirby feel about young, teenage girls getting pregnant?
10. a) When Kirby confronted Sol while he was mayor, how did he feel?
    b) Why did he feel this way?
11. What are the consequences of selling drugs?
12. a) Which character did you most identify with?
    b) Why?
13. How would you respond to someone murdering your best friend?
14. Besides for Midnight Basketball, what is another solution to keep young people off the streets?